COLLIDE

Ella Adams

Published by Little Blue Books, 2016.

Copyright © Ella Adams 2015

The right of Ella Adams to be identified as the Author of the Work has been asserted by her in accordance with the Copyright, Designs and Patents Act 1988.

All rights reserved. No part of this publication may be reproduced, stored in a retrieval system, or transmitted, in any form or by any means without the prior written permission of the author. You must not circulate this book in any format.

All characters in this publication are fictitious and any resemblance to real persons, living or dead is purely coincidental.

BAD BOY BILLIONAIRES SERIES

COLLIDE - a scorching romance featuring an irresistible bad boy billionaire that begins with a spilled cup of coffee on the streets of New York.

RIVALS - a sizzling Italian billionaire love triangle featuring not one, but two smoldering bad boys.

INDULGE - a sexy romance about a woman who choses to indulge her heart's desires by sharing TWO billionaires.

RESIST - a heart-stopping romance featuring one truly irresistible bad boy billionaire.

Books are standalone and can be read in any order

Part 1

Chapter 1

The day I met him, I was taking a cab to work and I was late.

New York City is not the easiest place to be for someone who is running late.

"Can you go any faster?" I asked the cab driver who was already in an irate state from my backseat driving through heavy traffic all the way uptown.

"Maybe. If I had a hovercraft. Can't you see it's not moving," he shot back at me, bad-tempered.

I sighed. I was going to be very late.

I worked at a high-end day spa just off Fifth Avenue that boasts the latest in organic and natural treatments. It was a beautiful place to work and we had most of the city's finest as clients.

I had been there for a couple of years and worked my way up from masseuse to operations manager, which gave me a little more leniency.

Something I was grateful for right then.

The cab inched forward along Park Avenue.

"Just let me out here; I'll walk the rest of the way."

I fumbled through my wallet, handing him some cash then searched my purse for my work key fob, as I was always losing it and wanted to make sure I had it before exiting.

My phone rang and I was soon juggling my purse, keys, change from the driver, as well as my ringing phone while trying to get out before the lights changed.

I didn't remember opening the door with a lot of force, but the sound on the other side let me know that I must have.

There was a loud thwack.

My mouth dropped open and my eyes grew wide. I stepped out quickly to see a heap of dark grey expensive suit bent over on the Park Avenue sidewalk.

Dammit, I had just knocked over someone passing by!

"I'm so sorry. Are you okay? I'm so sorry," I spluttered as I threw everything into my bag and ran toward the person.

Recovering his balance, a guy looked up at me, and my heart stopped for a few seconds.

He was long, lean, and handsome and easily the most beautiful man I had ever seen. He looked back at me with his large brown hooded eyes, and my knees literally went weak.

Then, as I reached for his arm to see if he was OK, I felt an electrical charge rush through my veins.

I wanted to say something else but I couldn't. I just stayed rooted to the ground with his eyes locked to mine. Then ever so slowly his gaze went from my face down my body to my feet, and then back up to my eyes.

He stood up fully then and I realized he was tall and towered over me.

I looked up at him, eyes wide. I wanted to snap out of it, but I couldn't. I was ... hypnotized.

Finally the cab driver broke the silence when he yelled, "Hey lady! Are you going to shut the door or what?"

"Oh, I'm sorry yes," I said and turned to do so.

The cab quickly drove off and I turned my attention back to the handsome stranger.

"Again, I apologize. Are you hurt?"

"Well, maybe just second degree burns." His voice was low and smooth like velvet.

I looked down at his hand to see a crumpled empty coffee cup, then glanced at his suit and noticed he was now wearing that coffee.

I was mortified afresh. I'm sure the coffee was hot but to top it off that was obviously a very expensive suit. *Armani,* I guessed.

"Oh no, I ruined your suit. Can I take it to the cleaners for you? I mean, not right now obviously because you're wearing it ..." I babbled rapidly. "But maybe we could go somewhere, and you could take it off...."

His eyebrows immediately rose at this suggestion and his face softened with humor.

"I mean, that's not what I meant. It came out wrong ..." I was rambling and couldn't stop.

I tended to do that when I got nervous and this man made me all kinds of nervous.

Finally, I stopped jabbering on and fidgeting.

"It's fine really," he said, now wearing a grin that could stop traffic. "I have lots of other suits just like it. But the coffee, it's dead. I think you should definitely replace that."

I was confused. I cocked my head to the side, unsure of what he meant. Then he laughed and added, "Come on, you're buying me a cup of coffee."

"Oh. Yes, of course! I was just on my way to work, but we can pop into a Starbucks, and I can get you a quick cup. It's the least I can do for knocking you over with a car door. Are you sure you're okay?"

"I think I'll live. It's this way, follow me," he said pointing in the direction of Central Park.

He walked fast, like most New Yorkers, and I scurried in my heels to keep up.

His phone rang and he took it out of his pocket. "I'm sorry I'll have to take this, but please let's keep moving," he said as he touched the screen.

He walked and talked as I tried to keep pace. It was all business, but I couldn't figure out what exactly.

It could have been real estate maybe, or stocks because I heard the word 'yields' a lot.

We walked side by side, not talking, but every now and then he looked over at me and grinned.

It was a smile befitting a mega movie star and I was sure I was blushing. I stared down to the ground at my feet, making sure I didn't stumble and fall over myself.

Then I noticed a Starbucks on the opposite corner and sort of half motioned to it, but he was still on the phone and ignored me.

Okay Olivia, I thought, just follow the guy. You nearly knocked him out, and maybe he has this special stand he likes to go to.

It was very possible he was a coffee snob and enjoyed a particular type or blend. It was certainly obvious that he was very well off and probably liked things a certain way.

He finally hung up the phone and looked at me.

"I'm so sorry. I would never have taken that call if I knew I wouldn't be able to get them off. Anyway, we're here."

He stopped then in the middle of the sidewalk.

"We are?" I turned to look, and startled, realized we were in front of none other than The Plaza Hotel.

"Yes. Come on."

Chapter 2

I followed him inside the rotating glass doors to the lobby of the grand hotel.

I had never actually been inside before.

As soon as we walked in though, I wanted to stop and stare with my mouth agape.

The place was absolutely stunning.

"I don't understand. What are we doing here?" I asked.

He smiled at me and kept walking, "Getting coffee of course."

I was giddy at how mysterious this all was. A few minutes ago I was in a rush to work and now here I was with a handsome stranger in the Plaza Hotel.

I followed him into the Palm Court, a grand airy light-filled room bordered by mirrored doors and marble columns that gave it that palatial sense the hotel was famous for.

A large glass dome of yellow and green crowned the entire room giving the ambience of a garden conservatory. The furnishings were white and elegant, and plenty of plants and palms filled the room.

There were a few people having breakfast, but the restaurant was mostly empty in the late morning hour.

He pulled a chair out for me at a nearby table and I sat down. Taking the other chair, he stared at me with a mischievous smile on his face.

He really was beautiful. His full lips looked soft and his dark hair was thick and lustrous with one piece falling over his brow.

A waiter came over and my companion immediately took command, "Two coffees, please."

The waiter nodded and was off.

"I assumed you would want coffee but perhaps that was presumptuous of me - to assume to know what you want," he said, eyeing me intensely.

He it in such a way that made me feel instantly aroused. Because I knew well that he was no longer talking about coffee.

What was going on here? Did this man find me desirable? If so, that was a first for me.

Handsome rich men never hit on me. This was way out of my comfort zone.

"Yes, I do like coffee," I mumbled, trying to hide that I was blushing.

I could feel him staring at me. So I gave myself permission to look back at him.

We locked eyes directly then and I was feeling all sort of unfamiliar emotions while he stared at me.

He was a complete stranger yet I wanted him to lean across the table and kiss me.

I wanted to know what he looked like under that suit, and ... just as quickly, I forced myself to stop thinking these thoughts and stop being an idiot.

"Here we are, two coffees," the waiter interjected, bringing me back to reality. "Will there be anything else I can get for you?"

"No, that is all thank you."

The beverages were presented elegantly in fine white and blue china. A caddy was placed in the middle with a small silver jug of milk and a small silver bowl with sugar cubes and silver tongs.

It was elegant and refined and it made me realize with a gulp that I was buying. That was the deal I had made for spilling coffee on him. This would probably be twenty dollars, if not more. I was glad I had just got paid.

Then it hit me. Work.

"I'm so sorry; I need to make a quick phone call. Will you excuse me?"

"Yes, of course. Take your time," he said.

I got up from the table and walked to the main lobby. I could feel him watching my behind as I walked away clutching my cellphone and the notion sent a fresh thrill through my body.

I made a quick call to the salon and made up an excuse. I said that I had a massive migraine but had taken medication so I would lay down and see if it went away and come in later.

It wasn't scheduled to be a particularly busy day so I figured it would be OK.

I walked back into the Palm Court and the mysterious stranger was still staring at me. He followed me with his eyes all the way back to the table.

The way he looked at me made me feel like he was undressing me with his eyes. It was unsettling yet tremendously exciting.

I sat back down.

"Do you like cream in your coffee?" he asked then.

"Yes, just a little."

Reaching across, he poured a small amount in my cup and whispered "Like that? Is that how you like it?"

What the hell? The way he said those words ... I could feel myself getting wet.

Make no mistake, this was foreplay.

And despite myself, I loved it. "No, that's perfect. Thank you."

He smiled innocently. Though I was pretty certain he knew perfectly well what he was doing.

"Sugar?"

"Just one."

He grabbed a sugar cube delicately with the tongs and placed it in my cup.

I picked up the little silver spoon and gave it a stir, then put the cup to my lips and looked over the rim at him as I sipped the hot liquid.

He stared at me and bit his bottom lip, his eyes flaring with what I now understood was desire.

I didn't know what was happening, but I wanted to find out.

I swallowed a mouthful of hot liquid, growing more and more excited with each exchange.

This was the most delicious coffee I had ever had in my life.

For more reasons than one.

Chapter 3

"Do you like it? The coffee?" he asked then.

"Yes, I do. It's delicious."

"Good. I'm glad you approve."

It's The Plaza, I thought. How could I not approve?

We sat in silence and he stared at me the entire time as I drank. I wanted to open my mouth to ask him a few questions, but I knew once I did I would get nervous and start rambling.

So I didn't. I enjoyed the way we were, just staring at each other. It was intense and seductive. It made me feel like a temptress.

After a few minutes, we were both done with our coffees. I figured I should get the check and get going, as at this juncture I was starting to feel uncomfortable about what would happen next.

The waiter walked over to our table and said, "Would you like anything else?"

"Just charge it to my room. Thank you," the stranger said.

"Yes, sir."

I looked at him, confused. First of all I thought *I* was getting the check. Second, he had a room here?

Now I figured it out. He'd brought me here for one reason only. He wanted to get me to his room.

I looked at him and cocked my head to the side in a question.

He grinned and said, "I figured it would be easier to come here, since I need to change my suit anyway. I can't go about my day wearing a coffee stain, now can I?"

"Oh, yes. I suppose that...makes sense." I was still suspicious of his motives.

The waiter came over with the check and handed it him. He signed for it and left it on the table, then stood up and I stood too. Time to leave.

"Thank you for the coffee. I'm really sorry about the collision, and the suit."

"Aren't you coming upstairs?"

I froze for a few seconds, while he stood there, still looking at me with that cocky grin.

My eyes widened and my mouth opened a little. I had not expected him to be so forward, but of course he would be this confident.

What *didn't* he have to be confident about though?

Then I did something I wasn't expecting. For some reason, I played along.

"Do you think I'm that easy?" I teased, as I put my hands on my full curvy hips.

Looking the way he did he had every right to be presumptuous and it wasn't as if I'd be able to resist.

I *wanted* him to touch me. I wanted him to take command. I wanted him to devour me.

Still, I had to play a little hard to get. After all, I knew nothing about this man and he was asking me up to his hotel room.

After I answered, he moved in closer, and I instinctively took a few steps back. He put only a few inches between us and looked down at me, his large brown eyes locked with mine.

He pushed the hair out of my eyes and trailed his hand down my face and said, "I just want your company. Come upstairs with me. Please."

The back of his hand went down along my face. I couldn't believe it; he was touching me.

And I didn't want him to stop. I couldn't believe how much my body was betraying me just then, while my mind struggled to figure things out. I was completely in lust with this guy.

He was confident, demanding, everything I wanted to experience in a man. And I suspected he knew how to please a woman in ways I could only imagine.

I had spent the last few years so focused on getting my life together that I didn't have time to date.

Or really, I was just bad at dating. I always saw the guy's faults right away, so I never even made it to date number two. It was a serious problem.

But so much time had passed since I had a simple raw sexual encounter that I was starting to feel like less of a woman.

I needed to rebuild my confidence, and I needed a man, a real man, to ravage me.

He seemed like exactly the kind of man that could fulfill that desire. The way he came on to me already made me feel like more of a woman in one minute than I had in one year.

I was intrigued.

And incredibly turned on.

Chapter 4

We stepped out of the elevator onto his floor.

"How long are you staying at the hotel?" I asked.

"I live here," he replied simply.

"Oh, I see." Surely only millionaires - billionaires even - could afford residence at The Plaza.

Who the hell was I with? I stopped walking while I thought this through a little more, and I didn't even notice that I'd stopped.

He walked over to me like he had before, putting only a few inches between our bodies. Leaning in close, his breath caressing my ear he said, "I know you want me. I know you want me to fuck you."

I gasped. I was not expecting bedroom talk out here in public. Before he was even inside the room, let alone anywhere near me!

It was erotic and intoxicating.

Then he continued, "Tell me your name."

"Olivia," I said in a breathless whisper.

He paused and locked eyes with me, his large brown eyes looking down at me and continued, "You know you want me, Olivia."

He was right, and even the way my name came out of his mouth made me feel even more aroused.

But it wasn't just his looks; it was how he commanded the space he was in. He was a magnet, a lady's man, a man's man, and an all round charmer.

He moved his mouth across my lips then, brushing them lightly. His mouth was soft and I could still smell the coffee on his breath.

My hands seemed to have a mind of their own as they reached up and touched his chest. I wanted to feel him through the stiffness of his suit.

In truth, I had been daydreaming about it since the moment I saw him.

The fabric was thick and I could feel his hard chest under it. He must have seen this as encouragement because he put his hand on the small of my back and pulled me close to him so I could feel his cock against me.

It made me instantly wet to know that he was so hard and I gasped at his aggression.

He trailed kisses down my neck, then slowly licked my skin from the base of my neck all the way up to my ear and said, "I'm going to lick you until you scream, Olivia. You know you want it. You want me to taste you."

That was enough. Hearing him say that, I knew I was going to let him do things to me, *everything* to me.

He moved his hand down from the small of my back to my bottom, on to the hem of my dress, and kept going until his hand was resting on against my bare thigh.

Then his thumb was under my dress, rubbing lightly against the crease between my thigh and cheek.

The anticipation was building inside me and this simple touch was enough to make me drenched.

He covered my mouth with his and parted my lips with his tongue. His kiss was deep and passionate and his breathing was growing heavy.

"Do you want to put my cock in your delicious mouth? Slide it in and out?" he whispered between kisses.

I couldn't open my eyes and my voice was barely a whisper as I simply breathed, "Yes," wanting to do exactly that right there and then.

I'd almost completely forgotten that we were still in the hallway, a public place - when he moved his hand from the back of my thigh to the front.

I gasped again at the proximity of his hand to my center.

Then suddenly he pulled away and took a few steps back, leaving me standing there with my mouth open and desperate for more.

He looked at me and grinned with a confident smirk. I hated letting him have such power over me, but I couldn't stop it.

I was hypnotized by this man.

He turned his back then and starting walking to his room. I stood motionless, and then he glanced over his shoulder. "Aren't you coming?"

At that point, wild horses couldn't stop me. I took my first steps forward as I followed him down the hall. I was doing this.

I wanted to experience more, wanted to be rocked to my very core in orgasmic pleasure.

I believed this man could do that to me, and there was only one-way to find out.

Chapter 5

I walked into the room and put my stuff down on a nearby chair.

The suite was gorgeous. Massive with high ceilings and lush furnishings, fit for a king.

I crossed my hands in front of me, suddenly feeling like a scared virgin about to have sex for the first time.

In some respects I was all new to this type of behavior. I certainly had never been with such a sexually confident man.

He opened the drapes wide and let the mid-morning sunlight fill the room.

Then he turned to look at me. "Stand on the bed."

"Why?" I asked, looking over at the humongous King bed which looked as though it could easily fit five people.

"Just do it. I want to admire you from here," he said.

I looked at him, then back at the bed and finally went over to it. I took my shoes off and climbed on top like he'd asked, and stood there facing him.

"Good," he said. "That's good. Now take your dress off, slowly."

I swallowed hard. I wasn't especially comfortable about getting undressed like this in front of a man in so much daylight. I wasn't overweight but I was ... voluptuous, and a million miles from the wraithlike supermodel-type I'm sure this guy was used to.

I had expected I would come in here and he would rip my clothes off at close range in the darkness. Not this slow strip show that he seemed to want.

I tried to remember something my friend Lily had told me once, "Men like naked, no matter what it looks like. Naked is hot." Maybe she was right about that.

So I unzipped the side of my dress, took a deep breath and slipped it over my head. I held it in front of me for a minute, sort of covering me.

"Throw it on the ground," he ordered.

I locked eyes with him and then did as he asked. There I stood in my white lace bra and panties.

"Good, keep looking at me. Don't look away. Now take off your bra, slowly."

I continued to stare at him, then reached behind my back and unhooked my bra. I let it rest on my front for a few seconds, then I grabbed a shoulder strap and pulled it down my arm slowly.

Letting my breasts fall free for this man was invigorating.

"Your nipples are perfect," he growled.

I bit my lower lip, pleased. I was not used to being talked to like this. I don't think a man had ever said those words to me.

I truly felt like a desirable woman standing there, as his gaze drank in my full breasts and he moved his hand down along his thigh.

Or so I thought. Instead, he was in fact rubbing his rock hard cock beneath his trousers.

To my disbelief, it looked to reach all the way down his thigh.

I gasped.

By now, I was so wet I could feel it start to drip down my inner leg.

"Now take off your panties and throw them to me," he said. My eyes grew wide. It was the filthiest thing I had ever heard.

But I liked it, and again I was deliciously thrilled by all this.

How was this man able to be so effortlessly elegant and polite in day to day life, and yet be so dirty in the bedroom? He was more and more of an enigma with each passing moment.

Which merely made him all the more desirable.

I grasped the strings of my panties on my hips and slowly pulled them down.

They were wet - I could feel it in my hand- and suddenly I was embarrassed that this would reveal to him the effect he was having on me.

"Give them to me," he said in a sterner, booming voice.

The command scared and excited me at the same time.

I tossed them to him and as he caught them, his hand caressed the fabric.

He looked up and smiled, "So wet. Your body is ready for me. You want my cock in you so bad. Don't you?"

I realized he'd expected them to be wet; it was what validated him and encouraged him.

I nodded my head yes and licked my lips.

He smiled and said, "Say it, Olivia. Say you want my big hard cock inside you."

I paused, with my eyes wide until he repeated, "Say it."

I snapped out of it, doing as he commanded, "I ... I want your big hard cock inside me." I almost added 'please' because at this point I wasn't sure if I could wait any longer. My body ached for him.

"Well you're going to have to wait," he replied mischievously, "because I want to taste you first. Can I? Can I taste you?"

"Yes," I moaned.

"Lay down." He moved to the bottom of the bed as I did as he asked. Then he grabbed both of my feet and pushed them up toward my center, spreading my thighs apart.

I moaned at his touch. I was in ecstasy. I felt like a siren laying there; like a real sexual being, and it was electrifying.

I was sure I would orgasm even before he went any further.

He lowered his hands on either side of my legs, then bent his head, still keeping eye contact with me.

Then stuck his tongue out and deftly licked me from the middle of my cleft up to my clitoris.

I screamed out, just as he said I would. He moaned at my response, then he went to work licking every inch of my center. He moved his tongue along the creases of my inner thigh up and down and across to the other side, before eventually putting it inside of me, penetrating me.

I wiggled under him. It was more than I could bear. I don't know where he learned this, but I was grateful to his teacher.

"I want you to come in my mouth Olivia," he said between licks. "Are you ready to come in my mouth?"

I could barely get out a word between moaning and gasping, but whispered, "Yes, yes make me come, please. I want to come in your mouth."

He focused all his attention on my clitoris then, and put his lips on it, suckling it gently.

I yelled out. No, I screamed.

Between suckling, he applied pressure with his tongue moving it from side to side and with this maneuver, I came, crying out as he moved his mouth down to my opening.

He moaned as he drank while my entire body was tingling and shuddering. I had never had an orgasm so explosive before. I'm not entirely sure I'd actually *had* a proper orgasm before; it was so intense.

He came up then and stood up at the edge of the bed, still fully clothed in the Armani suit, which only added to my sense of wanton vulnerability.

I was completely naked while he was clothed and very much in command.

He grabbed my legs and wrenched my entire body to the edge of the bed, before unzipping his pants and unleashing his rod.

I gasped, now understanding why this man was so confident.

It was hard, smooth and huge, the very picture of perfection, like something from a Greek God.

I immediately wanted to put it in my mouth, but I was enjoying being told what to do and when.

So I just stared at it, my mouth opening slightly in anticipation.

He grabbed my hips and pulled me closer.

"I'm going to fuck you now Olivia," he told me, as I trembled beneath him. "I'm going to fuck you so hard."

Chapter 6

He reached down, grabbed his shaft and placed the tip just inside my opening.

I was breathing heavily by now, desperate (though slightly scared) to feel all of that inside me.

He looked down and moaned. "I wish you could see this view."

He moved the tip in a little more but not entirely, and slowly pumped his body forward, moving in little by little, teasing me.

He sighed and moaned as he watched himself do this, and frustrated, I spread my legs apart wider. I was desperate for him. I couldn't wait any longer.

I wanted it, *needed* it now, and I was so wet I knew it would feel like heaven when he slid in.

He looked down at me then, meeting my gaze with heavy-lidded eyes, and with one hard thrust drove his entire cock inside of me.

I screamed.

It took me a few seconds before I could even catch my breath. He'd gone deep, much deeper than I was expecting, and I thought I would have another orgasm with that one move.

He smiled with satisfaction at my response and grabbed my hips, "You're so wet. So tight."

With that, he rammed faster and faster into me, slamming his body against mine and I could feel the fabric of his suit on my skin as we collided for the second time that day.

I was close again. I put my hands out on the bed and grabbed the sheets in my fists. I needed to steady myself. I was losing myself to ecstasy with this man. My whole body was awakening to new feelings, new desires and I wasn't sure if I could hold out any ...

Then all of a sudden, he stopped.

I sat up, confused and more than a little frustrated. Smiling, he took a few steps backwards and said gently, "Come here."

I got off of the bed and went to him. He took my hand and rested it on his cock, massaging it, rubbing it.

Understanding what he wanted, I looked down eagerly.

It truly was magnificent.

Putting both hands around its huge girth, I massaged a little, then bent over and put the tip of it in my mouth, wrapping my lips softly around it.

He moaned as I did so and I went down to my knees and opened my mouth wider, letting more of him in, tasting myself on him.

I put one hand on the base of his shaft and used my tongue to run circles over the tip, wanting to give him the same kind of pleasure he'd given me.

He tilted his head back and put his hands in my hair as I slid his hardness in and out of my mouth. Over and over, listening to him respond.

Finally, he gasped, "Stop."

I complied.

"Stand up."

He took my hands and helped me to my feet, before leading me back over to the bed.

Finally, he began to disrobe.

First the jacket came off. He laid it ceremoniously on the chair, then unbuttoned his dress shirt down the middle. He took it off and then gently laid that too on the chair, as though it was of great importance that he took care of his clothes.

Next came the shiny black patent leather shoes and socks, then the pants, boxer shorts, and undershirt.

Now he stood before me, completely naked. I gasped at the magnificence of him.

His six-pack abs were tight, smooth and tanned, with just the right amount of dark hair trickling down the center. His legs were strong and hard with huge thick thighs. His arms were muscled, but not too big and a small tattoo snaked across his upper arm, but I couldn't make out what it was.

At that point I didn't care. All I wanted was him inside me again.

He walked over slowly and climbed onto on the bed, imprisoning me with his arms as he hovered above me. "You're beautiful."

"*You're* beautiful," I replied in a whisper.

He looked at me with a grin, before suddenly entering me again in one swift thrust that took my breath away.

First he moved slowly, sliding in and out. Wrapping his lips around my nipples, kissing and sucking on them.

He used one hand to prop himself up and the other to massage my breasts, as he said my name over and over between kisses, "Olivia...Olivia."

I loved hearing my name come from his lips; it was intoxicating.

Eventually, he grabbed my leg and propped it on his shoulder as he moved deeper inside me.

I figured this meant he was ready to come so I opened myself wider, accepting him. He thrust harder inside me, then finally he tensed up and moaned louder and louder.

Finally, he collapsed on top of me and I felt the full weight of his strong body.

His scent was intoxicating.

My own body was still sending small tremors all over as the last remnants of my orgasm spread through me.

I breathed heavily, slightly dazed by the amount of passion and built-up sexual tension I had just released.

It had been the most exhilarating encounter of my life.

Chapter 7

About two hours later, I woke up.

I opened my eyes, unsure where I was.

It took me a few seconds to remember and I gasped when I realized I was in a stranger's apartment inside The Plaza Hotel.

Everything he had done to me came flooding back - the demanding requests, they way he licked me, the way he moved inside me.

And I didn't even know his name.

I closed my eyes in embarrassment. What the hell had I just done?

I looked over then at the man lying next to me in bed. He stirred a little as I drank in his beautiful face and gorgeous body.

The panic I was feeling seconds before subsided the more I looked at him. He stirred again and let out a little moan before opening his eyes. Then he smiled, moved his head and laid it on top of my breasts.

I ran my hand through his thick hair, massaging it a little. I couldn't help it; after all it was part of my profession.

After a few seconds he said, "You are so good with your hands."

"Thank you, you are good with...everything."

We both laughed. It felt nice to add a lighter mood to this incredible surreal situation.

For me anyway.

"I'm starving. I'm going to order room service, would that be okay with you?" he asked then.

"That would be lovely. I must admit I'm hungry too. What time is it?"

I looked at the clock. It was just past noon. Damn, I thought. I really should get to work.

But I didn't want to. I wanted to stay where I was; in bed with this gorgeous man eating room service and letting him touch me.

So I decided that's exactly what I was going to do.

He rolled out of bed and I stared at his gorgeous naked body as he walked to the phone.

He winked at me as he began talking and ordering food.

I knew I should contact work again so I needed to grab my phone but I was feeling insecure again about my body.

I took a deep breath and forced myself to get out from under the sheets, hoping he wasn't watching.

I tiptoed over to the chair, shuffled through my stuff and took a few things out before finding my phone.

I grabbed it and headed back to the bed and under the covers. I didn't bother to look at my mysterious lover. It was better if I didn't know if he was looking at me.

I sent a text to my coworker letting her know that my migraine never went away and I would be taking the entire day off.

It wouldn't be a problem. I never took a day off. I was always very dedicated. I put my phone on the bedside table and looked over. He'd hung up the phone and now rejoined me under the covers.

"I hope you are hungry because I just ordered a lot of food," he said, as he nestled his body against mine.

I was completely confused by this man. It was as if he was a different person by the hour. It was completely out of my comfort zone to be so intimate with a complete stranger, but I was enjoying the mystery of him.

I began to caress his shoulders, eager to touch him again. I couldn't not because his skin was so tempting.

He moaned under my touch. "Those hands of yours, they're like magic," he said.

Then he rolled on top of me and kissed me and I realized immediately that he was already aroused.

As was I. I wrapped my arms around his neck and kissed him back. It felt incredible.

Then he rolled over, put his hands on my hips and propped me on top of him. I straddled his waist and smiled at his delicious hardness beneath me. Fresh shivers of desire shot through my body.

He reached down and cupped my buttocks, squeezing them. He pulled me forward and said, "Sit on my face."

My eyes opened wide. I had never done such a thing before. I hesitated a little and he smiled, "It's okay. I won't bite."

I did as he asked, moved forward and arched my body up, hovering just above his mouth.

He brought his tongue up between my legs and licked my slick cleft. I gasped in fresh ecstasy, as he licked me up and down like the frosting off a piece of cake.

I placed my hands on the headboard to steady myself as he stuck his tongue deep inside. He squeezed my bottom and I moaned, in complete ecstasy. Then he moved to my clitoris and pressed against it over and over.

It didn't take long before I was yelling out again.

Then, in one swift move, he slammed me back down onto the bed beneath him, and was inside me in seconds.

His manhood filled me and went deep as he moved in and out fast. I knew we needed to be done before there was a knock at the door from room service, and the excitement of knowing that at any minute we could be interrupted only put me on the brink of yet another orgasm.

"I love being inside you. You feel so damn good," he whispered in my ear. He grabbed me, holding my body tight, as he thrust himself harder and faster inside me.

I couldn't handle it anymore and soon I exploded into orgasm again. This must have set him off too, because he came just a few seconds after I did.

He stayed inside me for a moment or two, both of us enjoying the remnants of our orgasm, until there was a knock at the door.

He grabbed his pants and pulled them on, while I found my dress and wrenched it over my head.

He went into the sitting room to open the door and soon after I heard someone roll in the room service cart.

He signed for it and then the waiter was gone. Soon after he came back into the bedroom, looked at me and winked as he rolled in the cart, a huge spread full of an assortment of foods.

"I didn't know if you were a vegetarian, or vegan, or anything about you so I just ordered everything."

I laughed. "Thank you. Though I am not a vegetarian."

"Good. I like a woman who eats." He uncovered the silver domes from the platters. There was steak and eggs, pancakes, bacon, croissants, fruit, of course coffee.

I ate hardily and so did he. We stared out at the glorious view of Central Park and made light conversation as if we'd known each other forever.

After we ate, we were soon back in bed. He fed me strawberries and lounged lazily, happier than I'd felt in an age.

Before long we had dozed off again and it was nice and comforting to have his strong body spoon me.

A couple of hours later I woke up. He was still asleep but I figured it was time for me to leave.

I didn't want to go, but I couldn't stay here forever either. This was a chance encounter, a brief respite from the world. And I knew enough to realize that was it all it could ever be.

I gently moved his arm from around my waist as I slipped from beneath the covers.

"Where do you think you're going?" he mumbled.

I blushed a little. "I should probably get home."

He growled a little in resistance, but I got up anyway. He watched me as I dressed and grabbed my things, a strange look on his face.

Then eventually, he got up too. "I'll walk you out."

My heart felt a little heavy as I realized that this most enjoyable encounter was finally coming to an end.

It was only when I reached the door of the suite that I realized I didn't even know this stranger's name. I chuckled a little at the absurdity of it all.

"What's so funny?" he asked, smiling too.

"I don't even know your name."

He put out his hand for me to shake it, irresistibly charming. "Troy."

"Hello, Troy."

"Hello, Olivia."

Then he stopped shaking my hand and once again pulled me into his strong arms, his breath hot and hungry in my mouth as he kissed me.

Eventually I pulled away, although it was killing me to do so.

I didn't want to let this guy - Troy - go, not to mention the incredible feelings he incited in me.

Finally I mumbled, "Thank you for a lovely ... um ... stay, and sorry again about our ... collision."

Though I was of course referring to the incident with the taxi that morning, I suddenly realized that it was the perfect metaphor for what our bodies had been doing all day.

Chapter 8

That night I lay in my bed replaying everything that had happened. I went from rushing and being late to work, to the happy accident of colliding with this handsome mysterious man.

Having coffee at The Plaza and then spending the day indulging myself in a drawn-out sexual experience shook my world.

It was unlike anything I had ever experienced in my life. I was extremely happy. I knew that this was a one-time thing and I was okay with that. I would never see Troy again and that was fine. It was probably better to keep it all a mystery anyway.

I fell asleep with a smile on my face.

A few days had passed and I was still thinking about my encounter with Troy though. Flashes of him naked would cross my mind.

I kept hearing his voice commanding me to do things and when I did I was instantly aroused. I spent the days like this.

Something had happened to me. I had changed. I was walking with a sexy sway to my step, I paid more attention to my appearance and felt like a siren. I felt fantastic, vibrant, and happy.

I went to work that day feeling excited about life. I was speaking to a customer about a new massage oil we had in stock when I felt a presence behind me. The hair on the back of my neck stood up.

"Hello Olivia."

I immediately recognized the voice, but it couldn't be. How could it?

I turned to see Troy standing there. He was in yet another dark Armani suit. I stared at him and he flashed that gorgeous grin.

"Hello." I handed the product to the customer and said to her, "We can ring you up at the front." Then I turned my attention back to Troy.

"What are you doing here?"

"I have an appointment."

I gave him a suspicious look. I knew that as a resident of The Plaza he could book an appointment here at any time, but I would play along. "Oh, is that so?"

"Yes."

"Well, in that case follow me."

I took him over to the front desk. "What time is your appointment?"

"Three," he said.

I looked it up in the reservations and saw that he was down for a massage with Amber.

She was gorgeous; a tall blonde from Sweden, with an accent, large breast, and a tiny waist - basically every male's fantasy.

A surge of jealousy came over me. I did not want Amber touching Troy. Furthermore I didn't want him to take a liking to her and maybe invite her back to his suite.

So I lied. I deleted Amber's name and replaced it with my own.

"Well, it looks like you are actually *my* three o' clock."

He grinned at me and I wondered if he guessed what I had just done.

A few minutes later he was laying face down on a massage table in front of me with nothing but a towel covering him. I was instantly aroused. I wanted him. I wanted him to touch me again.

It was going to be hard to concentrate on my work.

I poured warm oil in my hands and began to massage him. I worked on his strong shoulders and back. I rubbed him and kneaded him. He moaned a few times and it was an immediate flashback to our sexual encounters. I stopped.

"Is everything all right?" he asked.

"Yes, just getting more oil." I lied. Without warning Troy turned over onto his back. He grinned up at me and when I looked down I saw that he was rock hard. Completely naked on my table and unashamedly rock hard.

I gasped.

"I know; that's what you do to me."

I sighed at the sight of him. He was such a gorgeous, stunning creature. I massaged his chest and before I knew it, I'd slowly trailed my hand down to his cock.

He moaned.

"Shhh..." I warned him. I could get fired for this. Anyone could walk in the room.

Still, I wrapped my hands around his cock and gently massaged it. His breathing was faster and heavier and I could tell he was resisting the urge to call out in ecstasy.

Then he sat up and grabbed me. I gasped at the aggressive way he kissed me. He ran his hands all over my body and I melted in his arms.

He reached down and pulled up my uniform and his hands slid down over my panties. He used his fingers to push the fabric aside and pushed two fingers inside me. I forced the moans to not come out of my mouth. It was hard for both of us to be quiet, especially when our first encounter was so verbal.

Then he stood up from the massage table and got behind me. He grabbed my panties, yanked them down to my thighs and then entered me from behind.

I bent over the massage table enjoying the feel of him buried deep inside me. He slammed against my body, and I worried that the neighboring rooms could hear the smacking contact of our skin.

But it didn't worry me enough to stop. I couldn't even if I wanted to. I was in deep — literally, in the threshold of lust and passion. The excitement that we could get caught only made me more excited and closer to the brink.

I felt Troy rest his face on my back, he was using me to bury his mouth and stop himself from yelling out.

I too buried my head on the table and bit down on the towel. I climbed higher and higher and finally came.

My whole body shuddered as sheer ecstasy flowed through me. Troy moved fast and faster, sliding in and out. Then he finally exploded inside of me.

After a minute or two, he pulled out and sat back down on the table. I looked at him in disbelief. I couldn't believe this man was back in my life and at my place of work!

"Tell me how you knew I would be here?" I asked cutting to the chase.

"I saw the symbol on your key chain," he grinned wickedly. "I walk by here every day. I put it together when I noticed the place as I passed by yesterday."

"I'm glad you found me."

"Me too," he said kissing me.

I looked at the clock then and realized our hour was up. I needed to get Troy out of here before anyone got suspicious.

"Hour's up," I said pointing at the clock.

I gave him a robe and the opportunity to get cleaned up and then walked out of the room.

With a new spring in my step.

Chapter 9

Over the next week, Troy came back three more times.

Every time we had yet another even more passionate encounter in the massage room.

When he left I couldn't think about anything else except my next meeting with him. I thought about him constantly.

I was becoming infatuated. The way he made me feel was unlike anything I had ever felt before. I wanted more and more of it.

I knew nothing serious would ever come of this and it was just a sexual affair with no future.

However, I still couldn't get him out of my mind. I wanted this to be my life. This was the type of passion I had always wanted.

And now that I'd experienced it, I couldn't live without it.

One afternoon I was having coffee with my girlfriend, Lily. I told her that I needed to take charge of my romantic state.

I didn't tell her why, only that I was tired of not being in a relationship. She offered to help me out and set me up on a blind date with one of her coworkers that she thought I might like. I welcomed the offer.

I needed the distraction. I needed anything to get Troy out of my mind, before I was in danger of doing something stupid like falling in love with him.

The night of my blind date I loathed getting dressed.

It all felt so forced. I wanted to be excited and enjoy myself but the image of the powerful and gorgeous and Troy kept popping up in my mind.

I wanted him again and again, and not just sexually. I wanted to be with him. Those feelings were especially terrifying to me.

I curled my long brown hair and donned red lipstick to match my red and black dress. I wore black thigh high stockings and black stiletto heels. I wanted to feel attractive and enticing at least, if not for my date, then for myself.

Troy did that to me. I now saw myself as a sexy vixen and it was starting to show in how I dressed and presented myself. It was a refreshing change to my usual fumbling and rapid talking self. I liked it.

I topped my outfit off with a gold shimmering purse and a cropped black jacket. I was ready.

I took a cab to 57th street. I was meeting my blind date Ryan at The Russian Tea Room for dinner. The taxi pulled up and the doorman opened the door. I hesitated and took a deep breath feeling uneasy about the night, and then I stepped out.

Then I heard, "Olivia?"

I turned to see a handsome man with blonde hair and blue eyes dressed in a dark suit waiting for me. He was tall and well built and smiled at me with genuine warmth.

"Hi, you must be Ryan."

"Yes. You look very beautiful."

"Thank you," I said, feeling good and confident about his compliment.

We walked in and were escorted to a booth.

We faced the open room and I took in all the elegant furnishings and décor. It was a great place for a date. The atmosphere was dark and romantic.

We started with a few glasses of red wine, which helped loosen me up a little.

Ryan was nice and interesting and very well mannered. Though there was something about him that wasn't making me feel butterflies, and I couldn't figure out what it was.

The night went on in polite conversation while we ate our meal. I learned about his field in advertising, on Madison Avenue and his background in Connecticut.

On paper, he was the perfect man, husband material even.

Still, I kept finding myself comparing him to Troy. I compared the way he talked, the way he carried himself, the way he flirted with me, and even the way he lifted the glass to his mouth.

I silently kicked myself for not being able to get Troy out of my mind. I forced myself to give Ryan all my attention over and over again.

But after a few minutes I was right back to thinking about Troy. Oh no, I thought to myself. I've got it bad.

We finished dinner and Ryan recommended heading over to the bar at the Four Seasons for a nightcap.

Normally I would have suspicions about a man inviting me to any hotel for drinks after a date, but I didn't feel like that with Ryan.

He seemed like an all around nice and respectful guy that wouldn't try to pull something. What was really shocking about this was that I found it disappointing.

What was happening to me? I was craving that bad boy behavior. I wanted to be seduced, I wanted to be finagled into going to a man's hotel room and then being enticed to fuck him. I wanted the excitement and anticipation of it all.

It was completely not like me, or the old Olivia. The woman I was before I met Troy was gone.

We walked the few blocks to the Four Seasons, and I did my best to not search the streets for Troy when we passed by The Plaza Hotel. It was consuming me.

I decided the only way to give Ryan my full attention was to get drunk.

When we finally reached the Four Seasons I ordered whiskey straight up, which I think shocked my date. He couldn't know the inner turmoil I was fighting though and I needed to numb it.

Finally after two whiskeys I was loosening up. I even found myself putting my hand on Ryan's thigh when I laughed and playing with my hair a bit.

He was a handsome man and he was into me. Something that was refreshing at this point in my life.

But then it happened.

I saw him.

Chapter 10

I was sitting at the bar with Ryan. I was turned sideways, resting my elbow on the bar and fully facing my date.

Something caught my eye in the main room.

A red dress, mostly because it was almost like the one I was wearing. I turned slightly to check it out as the woman walked to the table. Then my mouth opened.

Escorting the woman in the red dress was Troy.

He had his hand on the small of her back, and they were clearly on a date. My heart dropped to my stomach.

It took me a few seconds to process what was happening. It was really him, in the flesh, and he was with another woman. I would have stared stunned like that for ages, but he turned his head in my direction, or I should say in the direction of the bar.

I quickly pulled my gaze away and swept it all the way back to my date. I was hoping this looked like I was merely looking around the room and not at Troy.

I had a feeling I was unsuccessful, but at least it was an attempt at covering up my disbelief and heartbreak.

I smiled at Ryan.

"Is anything wrong?" he asked.

"Oh no, not at all. I just thought I saw someone I knew. Should we have another drink?"

"Sure, another whiskey?"

"Yes absolutely." I laughed and put my hand on his thigh. If Troy did see me and was watching, I wanted him to know that I too was on a date.

The next fifteen minutes were excruciating. I could feel my back getting hot, like someone was burning a hole in it.

I wanted to turn and look to see what was going on, but I didn't. I wouldn't give him the satisfaction of knowing how much it bothered me to see him there with another woman.

I know I wouldn't be able to hide the hurt on my face if I locked eyes with him.

I made a good show of flirting with Ryan. I touched him, I laughed a lot, and I made constant eye contact with him and leaned in close when we talked.

But it was no use. I was feeling empty and hollow inside. I felt a lump in my throat and knew that tears would surely soon follow. So I excused myself to the ladies room to pull myself together.

I stared at myself in the mirror feeling really upset. I looked at my hair, now thinking it dull and lifeless. I stared at my brown eyes wishing they were blue. I turned sideways and stared at my shape in the mirror; basically scrutinizing everything about myself.

Troy had given me confidence, and now he had just as easily stripped it away. I was a mess. I turned away from the mirror and decided I should just end my blind date and go home. I was not in any place to continue faking it.

I stepped out of the ladies room and ran straight into him.

Troy looked down at me with those big brown eyes and said, "Who is that?"

"My date." I looked up at him and struggled to hide my surprise and sadness. I don't think I was successful.

"I don't like it."

"I don't care. You seem preoccupied anyway. Now if you'll excuse me, I need to get back to him." I tried to step around him, but he cut me off.

I moved to the other side and he blocked me again. I was his prisoner. He came closer and pinned me against the wall. My knees went weak.

This is exactly what I wanted from him, but the fact that it was happening seemed surreal.

He leaned down brushing his mouth against my ear and whispered, "You're mine. You know you're mine."

I moaned in response. I couldn't help myself. He covered his mouth on mine and kissed me. It was a deep, possessive kiss.

He moved his hand to my waist and pulled me against him. I tilted my head back surrendering. His other hand cupped my bottom as he squeezed and massaged it. I almost forgot we were in a public space and that anyone could walk into the hallway.

Then I pushed him away. "Why are you doing this?"

He didn't answer. He just smirked at me, then grabbed my hand and led me down the hallway and into the hotel lobby.

I needed to stop him and get back to my date. Or at least say goodbye to my date, but it was too late. I couldn't stop the momentum.

This is exactly the kind of effect he had on me. All the things that would normally matter to me just slipped away where Troy was concerned.

I took risks with him, at work, in my personal life and now here I was, ditching a perfectly good date.

Chapter 11

We stepped into the empty hotel elevator.

As soon as the doors closed, Troy stabbed the top floor button and then pushed me against the wall.

Kissing me hard, he moved his hand along my bottom to the back of my thigh, then picked my leg up, supporting it under his knee.

He moved his body between my legs and I felt his rock-hard cock against me. I felt even more aroused just knowing that he was so hard. It felt good knowing that I still had that effect on him.

He trailed kisses down my neck and along my cleavage. He licked the tops of my breasts and I put my hands in his hair, lightly tugging it.

The elevator bell sounded and we quickly stopped and separated, making ourselves presentable in case there were people on the other side of the doors.

The doors opened and there was no one standing there.

Troy looked at me and smirked that gorgeous grin that melted my heart. He grabbed my hand and led me into the long empty hallway.

We stopped in front of a door. He looked both ways down the hall. We were alone.

"Step into my office."

"What?" I was confused as he put his hand on my back and led me through the door. Suddenly we were in the maid's closet and laundry room.

"What are you doing?" I asked.

"Shhh..." He put his hands on my hips and picked me up and propped me on the washer which was currently on the spin cycle.

The vibrations shot up through my body as Troy reached down and opened my thighs. He fingered the fabric of my panties and pushed them to one side.

Within seconds his head was down between my legs and he licked my slick cleft as machine vibrated beneath me. I gasped.

He used one hand to hold my panties to the side while he licked, then touched himself with the other. I was in complete ecstasy.

It was late so the chances of a maid walking in were very slim, but still the danger of it was exciting.

He moaned and said my name. "God, Olivia."

I loved hearing that come from his lips especially in a moment of passion. It was music to my ears.

I had been dreaming of this for the last few days and now it was happening. I needed this. I needed him, he was my drug and I was addicted. I was now getting my fix.

I looked down at him trying to burn this image of him between my legs in my memory so that I could revisit it later when I needed another fix. He was incredible and my anger over him being with another woman had since left me.

After all he didn't go home with her. He was with me. That was a satisfying feeling. The vibrations from the washer got more intense and that was enough to send me into climax. A few seconds later I was yelling out in ecstasy.

My body shuddered and I released into an intense orgasm. The pent up tension and emotional night I had experienced made for an earth-moving orgasm. I felt the wetness slowly move out of me. Troy moaned and began to drink from me.

"I love tasting you."

He stood up and unzipped his pants. He looked at me locking his brown eyes on mine. He smiled and kissed me. I could taste myself on his mouth.

He reached down his pants and pulled out his hard rod and his manhood filled me while the washer vibrated against our bodies. His thick member moved in and out of me fast; this was a quickie, before we got caught.

"You feel so good. You are so tight," Troy whispered in my ear. He grabbed my waist and held me tight as he thrust himself harder and faster inside me.

I couldn't handle it anymore and I released again into another orgasm.

"You like that? Did it feel good? Tell me," he said as he continued to move in and out of me. He loved hearing me come.

"Yes. You feel good. Your cock feels incredible," I said in a soft low voice while I enjoyed my orgasm. Troy moved faster and escalated to the brink. He buried his face in my neck to cover his increasing loud moans. Then without another loud gasp of my name, he climaxed too.

Afterwards he relaxed and kept his head on my neck and stayed inside me. I rubbed my hands on his back feeling the strength of him.

We stayed locked together like this for a few seconds when the washer stopped. We laughed lightly at the absurdity of it, then suddenly, the door opened.

The look on the maid's face was one of shock and then she shook her head and slammed the door shut. It all happened in a matter of seconds. We didn't have time to even move from our locked positions.

As soon as the door was shut we jumped into action. We could not stop laughing as we pulled ourselves together. However, we did not want to get arrested either.

So we moved fast. We flew down the hallway and into the elevator, hoping that we wouldn't be stopped in the lobby. When the doors opened we walked with our heads down and moved fast. Then made it out onto the street and breathed a sigh of relief.

"Well, that was exciting," he laughed.

"Yes, it was fun."

"I don't want this to end, Olivia. Will you come with me to my place?" he looked at me with those incredible eyes and I couldn't resist.

But right at that moment I heard someone else call my name.

"Olivia?"

I turned to see Ryan in the process of hailing a cab in front of the Four Seasons. I was mortified.

I had completely forgotten that I was on a date.

Chapter 12

"Ryan...I " I immediately felt horrible.

I glanced at Troy and then back to Ryan who looked at us both and seemed to immediately understand the situation.

"I'll be right back." I whispered and walked over to him, biting my lower lip in embarrassment.

"What's going on? Did you really just ditch me in there for another guy? Is that really happening? Unbelievable," he said, shaking his head in disapproval.

"I'm so sorry Ryan. It's a long story. It's not what it looks like. I mean I guess it is. There's just so much ... it's hard to explain."

"That doesn't matter. Whatever the story I might have understood, but you got up and just left me there. That's the worst behavior. I should never have let Lily set me up with you if I knew you were this kind of person."

"But I'm not. Really I'm not. It's just..."

"Actions speak louder than words Olivia," he said as he opened the cab door and stepped in. He slammed it behind him.

I stared at him as the cab rolled away. He was right. I was behaving like a horrible person, a selfish woman. And though I had never been that person before, and was generally a quiet and nice girl, even too nice, that didn't matter to Ryan. What he saw and experienced just now was the Olivia he thought I was.

I was guilty of being rude and slutty. I felt frustrated and ashamed, but knowing that Troy had just invited me to go to his place kept my energy up.

I would think about the Ryan incident later, especially when I would have to answer to Lily about it.

For now I would continue to enjoy myself. This is what I wanted, and yes I was going to be selfish and enjoy it.

I turned back toward Troy then, only to find that he was not standing there anymore.

I turned and scanned the sidewalk but I could not find him. I started to panic, but then I saw him. Talking to a gorgeous woman - the one he was with in the bar. I flushed. I didn't know what to do.

Should I walk over to them, or turn and walk the other way with my tail between my legs?

No. I wouldn't do that. If I walked away I would regret it. At least if I approached it would answer all the questions I would have if I left. Questions that would inevitably drive me crazy.

I approached and stood right beside him, and smiled at the woman, trying to come across confident, though my insides were churning.

Troy looked over at me. I couldn't distinguish the look on his face. He didn't smile but he didn't look angry either.

Finally the woman introduced herself, "Hello. I'm Jessica," she said.

She had an odd knowing look on her face that I tried to not notice.

"This is my work colleague," Troy said gesturing toward her.

"Oh, nice to meet you." I smiled and tried to pretend I didn't notice the awkward tension "I'm Olivia."

The woman smiled an obviously fake smile and said, "Well it was nice to run into you Troy, and nice to meet you Olivia. I must rejoin my friends inside. Excuse me."

He nodded at her and then grinned as he turned toward the street with his arm around me.

He kissed my neck and touched my thigh. The appetite on this man, I thought to myself.

I wanted to ask him about the woman, Jessica. Clearly there was something going on there, but I was riding the high of him being in my arms and didn't want to ruin it.

We walked to his suite. The Plaza was busy and bustling as usual. I felt like a trophy wife as he escorted me through all the elegantly dressed people. I could get used to this.

We made it to his room and to my shock we didn't go straight to the bedroom.

"Make yourself at home," he said as he took off his jacket and shoes.

Okay, well I guess I would make myself at home.

I went to the bathroom to freshen up. Then I gasped at what I saw in the mirror. My hair was disheveled and my red lipstick was smudged around my mouth. I looked like a clown.

Clearly I was freshly sexed and I had talked to Ryan and Jessica looking like this. I was mortified at the thought.

I took out my make up bag and freshened up, then straightened my thigh high stockings and took off my heels.

Then I rejoined Troy in the sitting room portion of the suite.

I was astonished at what I saw. He was curled up on the couch with a blanket and TV remote in hand. Were we really just going to hang out?

"Are you hungry? I'm famished. I ordered dinner, I hope you don't mind," he said.

"Yes, I am hungry. I had quite a bit to drink and it would be nice to eat something."

"Good. Come here," he said opening one end of the blanket. He was shirtless in boxer shorts and inviting me to snuggle under the blanket. I got on the couch and cuddled up next to him.

"Who was that guy? I didn't like seeing you with anyone else."

"Ryan. He's just a guy I'm seeing. Or was until you pulled me away." I didn't need to tell him it was a blind date. I wanted him to know I had other men pursuing me. Even though I obviously would never hear from Ryan again.

Besides, his jealousy felt good.

"I don't like it. Just know that."

He picked up the remote and started flipping through the channels and found an old black and white scary movie. I snuggled in closer to him feeling in complete bliss.

A half hour later our room service dinner arrived. However it wasn't just a regular room service cart. It was dressed with lit candles and roses. I looked at Troy who winked at me. He signed for it and closed the door.

"I figured if we were going to dine in I could at least make it a romantic late night dinner."

I got up from the couch and kissed him. "That's very sweet. Thank you."

We sat on the couch and he took the silver domes off all the platters. There were two steaks, two lobster tails, mashed potatoes, a pot of hot coffee, and two slices of cake. It was an interesting assortment of foods.

That thought must have shown on my face because Troy looked at me and said, "I know. Strange layout, but I was craving comfort food like mashed potatoes. My grandmother used to always make those and I like to eat them late at night under a blanket. The lobster, well I've been thinking about going to my house in the Hamptons or even taking a sail up to Maine. Thinking about that made me crave lobster. You should come with me to the Hamptons soon. Before it's unbearably cold and we won't be able to enjoy ourselves on the beach."

I looked at him. It didn't escape my attention that he said "we" and that he was inviting me on a trip to his house. I tried to not let these things pull at my heartstrings so I went back to focusing on the food. "Well, those descriptions has me craving those foods too. How lucky am I that they are right in front of me."

Troy laughed and then said, "Coffee?"

"Yes, please."

He poured me a cup and I immediately flashed back to our first coffee together downstairs in the Palm Court. How erotic and exciting that was. I guess he thought of it too because he said,

"And do you like cream in your coffee? I can't quite remember."

"Yes, just a little." I said smiling at him. He poured a small amount and said, "Like that? Is that how you like it? Or do you want more?"

He was re-enacting our first encounter.

"No, that's perfect. Thank you."

"Sugar?"

"One."

He grabbed a sugar cube delicately with the tongs, kissed it lightly and then placed it in my cup. I laughed as he handed me the cup and picked up the little silver spoon and gave it a stir.

He chuckled a little. "Seems like only yesterday that you spilled coffee on me. Or I should say, almost knocked me out with the cab door."

I laughed. Then he took my hands and kissed the tops of them and my heart dropped to my stomach. This was such a change from the erotic bedroom talk of before. I kissed him back and then a loud scream came from the television. We both laughed at looked at the heroine on TV being attacked by a monster.

"Let's eat," he said.

We dug into our meals. Really dug in being messy and putting all elegance aside. It was a very comfortable feeling. I could get used to this, I thought.

I felt walls coming down on my side and on his too. I looked over at him and watched him watch the movie and enjoy his meal and enjoy my company.

I don't know exactly when I fell asleep, but a few hours later I woke up to Troy carrying me from the couch to the bedroom.

I looked up at him, my eyes barely focusing. He stared straight ahead and I reached up and wrapped my arms around his neck and pulled myself tight into his chest. He smelled so good.

"It's okay, go back to sleep," he whispered delicately.

It was all a haze as I was still mid sleep.

As soon as I hit the bed I fell back into a slumber.

Lots of whiskey and a food coma helped for easy sleep.

The last thing I remember was Troy fitting his body against mine and spooning me.

His warmth heated my entire body as I slept with a smile on my face.

Chapter 13

When I woke up the next morning it was eight o'clock.

I stretched out and moaned to the glorious morning. Then I remembered I had work today and I gasped and jumped out of bed.

I could hear the shower going and knew Troy must be in there. I rushed around and realized I was still in my going out clothes. My elegant red dress had stayed on me throughout the night.

That was a first, I thought. It was a wonder that he didn't try to peel it off of me.

I searched for my shoes and then heard a knock at the door. I hesitated, unsure what to do. I looked out the peephole and saw that it was room service.

Geez, how much room service could a man eat? I let the guy in and signed for it.

Just then Troy came out of the shower with a towel wrapped around his waist. It was a sight to behold. I looked at him up and down and wanted to walk over to him and lick the wet droplets off his chest.

I hated myself for being so easily aroused.

"Good morning. Oh good, coffee just in time." He uncovered the platters to reveal croissants, fruit, bagels and cream cheese.

"I really have to go. I'll be late for work and I have to go home and change."

"No, you don't."

He came over to me and hugged me from behind. The smell of his clean wet skin was intoxicating. He ran his hands down the front side of my body and I moaned in response.

"I really do have to go. I need to head home to change and then come all the way back up here. It's going to take forever."

"What if you didn't need to go home to change — would that cut some time out and you could stay a while?"

"Well, yes I suppose. But I can't wear this to work," I said confused.

He walked over to the phone and picked it up and said, "Transfer me to women's clothing. Yes, thank you. Hello, yes I'd like to order a few items and you can place it all on my account. To be sent over in half an hour - can you manage that? Great, hold on."

Then he handed me the phone and said, "It's Bergdorf. Order whatever you need."

Then he served himself coffee and walked to the bedroom. My mouth dropped open. Bergdorf Goodman - was he serious?

I ordered a pair of skinny jeans, a thin sweater, ballet flats, and a toothbrush then I hung up the phone, feeling like a princess.

I put my bag down, took off my shoes and made myself comfortable yet again. I poured some coffee and grabbed a croissant and joined Troy in the bedroom.

He was in the process of putting on a pair of boxers and I sighed at the sight of him naked. He was stunning.

"Get everything you needed?"

Not quite.

"Yes, thank you."

"Good."

He came over to me then and kissed me. His kiss was soft and slow. He put his arm on my lower back and then slid it down my buttocks. He cupped and squeezed and I moaned in response. It felt good and at this point I wanted it. I wanted him.

He moved his other hand on my chest. He unzipped my dress and moved his hand inside it. He found my breasts and squeezed and massaged them. We kissed and groped each other for a few minutes then I ran my hand against his chest, down along his belly and his taught abs.

I went further to his thigh and found his hard cock, caressing it up and down jerking him off through his boxers. He moaned and pulled away from me, then turned me around and pushed me over.

Knowing what was coming, I placed my hands on the bed. He pushed my feet apart with his foot and then peeled off my panties down to my ankles.

"Olivia. You are so hot. I want to fuck you. I want to fuck you hard."

I felt his mouth kiss my bottom and then trail little soft bites down along it further and further.

He got down on his knees, arched his back and stuck out his tongue to lick my wet cleft. I moaned in response and his hands grabbed my buttocks and squeezed and massaged while he had his tongue inside me.

He licked and moaned and said, "Now I want to taste you. I want to make you come on my face."

He moved his tongue to my clitoris and I gasped in response. He pressed against it and moved from right to left faster and faster.

Finally I was there. I yelled out. He moved his mouth over my opening and sucked on me, drinking from me. I couldn't believe how horny this was. And I couldn't believe how much I liked it.

Then he stood up and said, "Did you like that? Did that feel good?"

"Yes," I said in barely a whisper as I was still enjoying my orgasm.

"You're so wet now. You're wet and ready for me. Do you want my cock inside you?"

"Yes," I said.

"Say it. Say you want my cock inside you."

I breathed in deep and turned my head over my shoulder to look at him, he was smirking and his beautiful lazy grin turned me on.

"I want your big cock inside me. I want you to fuck me with your incredible cock."

He pulled his boxers down and with one swift move his hands were on my hips and the tip of his shaft was inside me.

He put his hands on my buttocks and held onto them, then pushed himself deep inside me. I yelled out in ecstasy. He was so huge and I couldn't control the volume of my voice even if I wanted to.

This time, Troy was slow about moving in and out of me. He knew he was big, and was careful to be gentle with such a weapon, especially in this position.

His hands cupped my breast and he fondled them as he circled his hips. I let out a soft whimper.

"Do you like it? Tell me you like it," he commanded.

"Yes, it feels so good. I like it, don't stop. Harder, please ... harder," I whispered.

With those words Troy obliged, slamming harder. Pounding me. He held onto my hips guiding me against him. He would pull out just enough, and then push hard again, and each time he went deep, he would stop and move in a circle a little before pulling away from me again. It was a pattern. A glorious pattern.

He continued to pound at me and the sound of our skin colliding was loud and made me even more aroused. I climbed higher and higher, and then eventually released into climax.

"Did you come?" he asked.

"Yes," I said barely getting the word out as my body convulsed in little tremors.

"Good, I want you to come again and again," he replied confidently.

My eyes widened. He wasn't even close to climaxing; he was going to go on and on...

I braced myself, trying to keep steady, though I felt like collapsing with weakness at the intensity of my orgasm.

For what seemed like fifteen more minutes - though I can't be sure since I had no concept of time - Troy continued to thrust in and out of me.

He would go slow and then speed up and stop, and then go again. I never wanted it to end I wanted to stay with him inside me forever. It was absolute heaven.

Then finally, without warning, one hand on my hip, he reached around with his other hand and put his finger on my clitoris. I yelled out. I was so sensitive and he massaged it lightly.

My screaming really turned him on, I knew. It was that cockiness in him, he liked being a sex god. The fact that he knew how to push a woman's buttons really got him going.

I cried out, "I'm coming." And with that he started to yell and moan. He moved in short fast movements in and out and I exploded into orgasm as I cried out.

Then finally, he came too.

Chapter 14

I left The Plaza that day in my new designer clothes and a happy mood. The next few days went by in a blur as I thought over and over about how we had spent a night in comfort in front of the television.

Two days had gone by and I had not seen Troy, but that didn't bug me. He knew how to find me at work, and after spending that night together I was certain we had something going.

I was expecting to be at his house in the Hamptons in no time.

I went about my days going to work and doing errands per usual. The problem with taking the subway in New York during cold and flu season is that your chances of catching it increase by one hundred percent.

I had soon become of a victim of the subway cold. I woke up with a horrible headache and the sniffles so I decided to call in to work.

I made myself hot chicken soup and tea and nursed myself back to health for the next three days. Nothing like a horrible cold to make you binge on romantic comedy movies.

Normally I would not want to admit this, but I felt that Troy and I had reached a good place, a different place.

I didn't know what that place was, but he was more present than he had ever been before. It was still just a sexual connection and I was okay with that, but something else was happening. I couldn't really explain what.

I went back and forth about how I felt about him. One day I would think I'm completely in love with him and the next, I would be completely fine with just the sexual encounters. I was becoming my own emotional roller coaster.

I spent the next three days in bed watching television and pondering these thoughts.

By day four I was feeling normal again. I stayed in the entire morning and slept late, but woke up feeling better.

It felt good to be out and about again. Being sick was the worst for me because sitting inside doing nothing made me depressed.

I was a New Yorker and I needed to be walking around and functioning in society. I just needed to get back to a normal structure. Being home from work for almost a week had given me an extreme case of cabin fever.

It was a beautiful sunny day with a slight chill in the air. I could see my breath as I breathed out and the steam from my coffee rose from my hand. I was in good spirits.

I walked around Manhattan, doing my errands and decided to go by my place of work to check in and let them know I would be back the next day.

I walked fast past The Plaza Hotel. I didn't want to feel like I was stalking, but it was on my way to work after all. I walked on the opposite side of the street near the Apple Store and I tried to look down at my feet and act casual.

But curiosity got the better of me. I looked over at the building and the people bustling outside, when a woman caught my attention.

I stopped in my tracks. I couldn't believe what I was seeing.

My co-worker Amber, the gorgeous Swedish masseuse that I envied.

She was walking towards the hotel entrance, and a man in a dark suit was leading her.

It was Troy.

Part 2

Chapter 15

I stood on the street in shock in front of the Plaza hotel.

My heart plummeted to my stomach. I started to feel a cold sweat cover my entire body. Feeling disbelief for what I had just seen was the only way of controlling my response reaction.

What were Troy and Amber doing together? It couldn't be what I thought, though there was no other explanation. They must be lovers.

I needed to get away. I needed to stop myself from running across the street and confronting him. I hailed a cab and got in. For a few blocks I sat in the back seat with the sadness welling up inside of me.

I fought back tears. How could he do this to me? Not only was he with another woman, but it was my co-worker. The one that made me feel the most insecure about myself. She was the exact opposite of what I was. She was the type of girl that could bring Troy to his knees. Maybe even lasso him into a relationship.

I was sick to my stomach. It was too much. I was raging on irrational and that's when I told the cab driver, "Turn around. Take me to The Plaza."

The cab turned back around and drove up Madison. I had no idea what I was going to do or say. I couldn't think. I only saw red. I was shaking with sadness and anger too. The cab pulled up outside and I threw a few bills at the driver not bothering to wait for change. I jumped out and made my way inside the hotel. My sight was blurry because of my watery eyes, but it didn't matter because I didn't bother to look up from my feet. I didn't care about anything but my broken heart.

I stomped my way down the hall and into the residential section. When I got to Troy's door I stood in silence. I heard nothing but I couldn't contain myself anymore. I formed a fist with my hand and pounded on the door. The door opened, on the other side was Amber.

"Olivia?" she said with a confused look on her face. Of course she was confused. She had no idea I had been involved with Troy. We did a very good job at hiding our secret sexual escapades that no one knew. It made me feel cheap for the first time.

"Where is he?" I said with my lips set in a hard line and tears flowing down my face. Amber was in complete confusion. She opened the door wide. Troy walked into view from the direction of his bedroom. He was in his boxer shorts and had a look of surprise on his face.

"Olivia? What are you doing here?" he said coming to the door.

I narrowed my eyes. I looked at him and then at Amber. At this point I think she got the message. I wanted to call him all sorts of names, but nothing came out. Instead I turned and ran down the hallway. Then the most embarrassing thing happened, I tripped and fell.

"Olivia," Troy called after me.

"What is going on here?" Amber asked.

I was embarrassed but I didn't care. I needed to get out of there. I was in full humiliation and heartbreak, but the rage blinded me to all of it. I just wanted to leave and never look back. I wanted to change everything about my life. I would go home, change jobs, and never see Troy again. I would get lost in the anonymity of New York City. I sat up and prepared to stand.

Troy was already kneeling at my side. "Are you all right?"

"Leave me alone," I said between moments of crying.

I tried to get up to my feet, but a pain shot up from my ankle up through my leg. I let out a whimper of pain and grabbed my ankle. This was the worst thing that could happen. Now I couldn't flee like I wanted to. I was stuck here.

"Is it your ankle?" Troy asked.

I wouldn't answer him. I was not going to address him. He was dead to me. I tried to get up again, and then again suffered the same pain and yelled out in agony. I crumpled to the floor and cried. I was defeated, humiliated, and helpless.

"You're hurt," Troy said as he put his hand on my ankle. His touch seared through my skin. Even in this pain, it felt good to have his hands on me. I hated myself for that. He reached down and scooped me up in his strong arms. His rescue mode made me feel like melting. The warmth of his bare chest was enough to make me forget that he had another woman in his suit. I could smell him and almost taste him. It only made the pain more severe. I wanted to say, "Don't touch me. Leave me alone," but I couldn't. I could scarcely breathe.

Troy brought me into the seating area and laid me on the couch. I buried my head in the side of it. I didn't want to look at either of them.

"Should I get some ice?" I heard Amber say.

"No, maybe you should just go." Troy said.

"Fine." She slammed the door on her way out and this made me feel a little satisfied. Though I couldn't ignore the fact that she was there at all.

Chapter 16

I looked up at him and he had that angry hard set to his jaw again.

He looked at my ankle and back at my face. He put his hand on my foot. I breathed in at his touch. I didn't know what was happening here. Then he slowly took off my heels. I was shocked at his gentleness with me.

"I'll get some ice." He left and went into the kitchen.

I was confused, but the pain forced me to do nothing but lay there. He returned and knelt down beside my feet. He looked perplexed though I couldn't figure out why. He was hesitant to touch my ankle again. He moved it slowly and said, "Does this hurt?"

"No."

"What about now?"

"No." I said noticing that he was speaking softly. It was making me aroused. I tried to push those thoughts out of my mind.

"I don't think it's broken. A sprain possibly," he said as he gently massaged it. I noticed his breathing had changed. He was intently focused on my feet. I watched him and feelings of lust flooded me. I wanted him. He stopped and cleared his throat and took his hands off me as though he remembered where he was. He grabbed the ice and laid it on my ankle.

"What are you doing here? Why were you pounding on the door?" he asked.

"I wish I knew. I was outside and I saw you with Amber. I saw you lead her inside and I was so angry. Why was she here? How long have you been sleeping with her?" I asked. I started shaking and tears again rolled down my face. I continued, "Why would you do that to me? She works with me."

"I know. I went in to see you, and you were out sick," he explained.

"And since I wasn't there you just pick another woman to have sex with? I was out sick, it's not like I had disappeared completely. I would have been back in a few days. How could you do that?"

He went over to the bar and poured two glasses of brandy.

"What really angers me is that you couldn't find comfort elsewhere? Why did it have to be someone I know? Why did it have to be my co-worker? There are millions of women in this city, Troy. You could have had the decency to not make this so complicated and hurtful for me by picking any one of those millions of women. Just not the ones in my immediate life, do you understand that?"

"You don't want me," he blurted.

I froze. How could he say that? I cared for him more than I should. It was obvious that it showed.

He handed me a glass of brandy and then gulped down another one. He was silent for a long time. He walked over to the window and gazed out. Then he said, "I just do what your body asks of me, and that is it. I'm sorry if I hurt you, I didn't mean to. You're right I could have taken my extra escapades outside of your life. I didn't think it through. I honestly didn't even think it would hurt you, because you show no amount of affection when you're with me. It's just fucking for you."

I stared at him wide-eyed. What had I gotten myself into? This was the worst thing that could happen. I had fallen for someone that couldn't read me emotionally. This would never work.

"I don't know anything about you. We never talk, you just want me for sex."

"What?" I was astonished.

"You disappear. The only way I know how to get a hold of you is to go to your place of work. You're a mysterious woman Olivia."

I wanted to throw up. The amount of pain from my ankle mixed with this extreme misunderstanding was too much to process. I wanted to protest and tell him he was the playboy here, not me. That he was the one that lured me into bed, he was the seducer not me, but I didn't. It was too much for now. I was concentrated on my rage and jealousy. But there was something else, the shift. Suddenly I felt powerful. I was the one in control now. It was intoxicating and it took hold of me unlike anything I had ever felt. It was power.

"Drink that. It will help with the pain. And numb everything else," he said pointing out the brandy in my hand. I drank it down and handed him the empty glass and said, "One more."

He filled my glass to the brim and handed it back to me. I drank it fast again. I wanted to feel drunk. I wanted to numb my heart.

"How long have you been seeing her?" I asked.

"I only just met her today. You interrupted what would have been our first... encounter," he said.

I felt some relief, though not entirely. I felt some satisfaction for having stopped things, but it didn't really matter. Troy would never be a one-woman man, and I needed to process that. I needed to get out now.

"I should go," I said. I took the ice pack off my ankle and sat up. As soon as I put my foot on the floor a searing pain shot up my leg. I yelled out. Troy was at my side immediately.

"Damn it, Olivia. Lay back. You can't walk. I won't let you hurt yourself simply because I'm an inconsiderate jerk. You have to stay off of it for the rest of the day."

Which meant I had to stay here, in his power.

Chapter 17

Troy laid me out on the couch and put the ice pack back on my ankle. He placed pillows under my head and covered me with a blanket.

"Don't do that. Don't take care of me. Don't be sweet to me. It's confusing," I said. I hated him. I wanted to hate him even more. I needed him to be a jerk to me so that I could hate him and never look back. I would leave this with all the power in my hands.

"Just because I'm a jerk doesn't mean I don't have compassion. I am still a human being and I care for you. I'm connected to you. I want comfort and stability like anyone else."

I began to cry. He kneeled down next to me and hugged me. It felt good.

He looked at me. We locked eyes. He was absolutely beautiful and my lips parted in response to him staring at me. He must have taken this as a sign cause he instinctively leaned in and kissed me.

I wanted him. Despite everything, I still wanted him. My body was already responding to him. His breathing was faster and heavier. He ran his hands all over my body. I melted in his arms. He reached down and pulled up my dress. His hands slid down over my panties. He used his fingers to push the fabric aside and pushed two fingers inside of me. I forced the moans to not come out of my mouth. He grabbed my panties and yanked them down to my thighs. I moaned, I liked the way I was being handled. I liked that I had no choice but to lay there. I couldn't exactly get up and walk away with my ankle the way it was. I was a prisoner.

He moved his head down and began to lick me. I gasped. He moved his tongue from the top of my cleft down to the center. Then he moved his tongue inside me. Penetrating me. I was in ecstasy. I could barely handle my aroused state. I no longer felt pain in my ankle only butterflies in my stomach and pulsing in between my thighs. He moved his tongue in and out of me while he moaned. I couldn't believe what was happening.

My mind was racing with thoughts until he moved his tongue to my clitoris, and all thoughts vanished from my mind. His tongue moved over it slowly licking it like a lollipop. He grabbed my panties again and pulled them all the way down. He was careful with my ankle and gently rolled them over it. He threw them on the ground. He came back up my body and put his head between my legs again. He used his fingers to spread me open so his tongue could reach further in. I closed my eyes and let him take me higher. I started to move, as I couldn't contain myself. His movements got faster and I was on the brink. Faster and faster he flicked with his tongue until I arched my back up and tensed. Then my whole body shuddered as I released into an explosive orgasm. I yelled out and grabbed onto the couch tightly. I needed it to steady my dizzy head. He stood up and towered over me. I looked up at him, feeling excited and frightened at the same time. He was so commanding over me. No matter what he wanted to do, I could not get up and leave with my hurt ankle. It was a scary and intoxicating feeling. I was helpless to stop him. He gently pulled my dress up and over my head and threw it on the floor. Now I lay before him in my bra and no panties. He stood up over me and let his gaze go from my head to my toes like he was scanning me. I felt vulnerable.

He pulled down his boxers. He stood naked in front of me. I felt like I was looking at a Viking warrior from the past. His broad shoulders were strong and well defined. His arms were strong and his chest was chiseled. His cock was large and perfectly pink and smooth. He grabbed it and stroked it a bit. I was entranced.

He reached down and took off my bra. He knelt down beside the couch and put my nipple in his mouth. He sucked and licked it gently. I put my hands in his thick brown hair. I had missed this. I needed this.

He stood up and placed his body on top of mine between my thighs. My eyes widened, this was happening. He grabbed his cock and placed it in my opening and slowly pushed it in. I yelled out. He filled me entirely. He reached deep inside me. He put his mouth over mine and kissed me. A passionate long kiss, then he started pumping his hips. He went in and out of me fast. I widened my legs opening them wider and wider. His skin smacked against mine. I was so aroused by him inside me mixed with the heavy emotions of it all, that I was almost on the brink again. He moaned and jerked his body left and right inside me. Then he paused and kissed my breasts, then started pounding me again.

Then with one last push and a loud groan he exploded inside me. He relaxed on top of me. We laid that way for a few minutes. Then he pulled out of me. He didn't say anything.

Tears welled up in my eyes and tears rolled down my face. The problem was, I had become addicted to being with him. It was a hopeless process.

Chapter 18

I spent the weekend nursing my sprained ankle and replaying the events that had happened. I was so upset and angry. I was angry with myself, and I was angry at Troy for not telling me sooner about his true feelings.

About how he saw me and what he thought of me. His perspective of me was so wrong. Though looking back, I guess I could see why he thought that.

I needed to stop focusing on him and focus on myself. I felt like I had lost myself to all of this. I needed to make a decision about work. What would I do? I couldn't face Amber, but I didn't want Troy to ruin my life either. So I put in a request to transfer to another branch of the spa. The anxiety was stressful and I hardly slept that weekend.

My friend Lily had come over to help with a few things since my ankle was still sprained. She had not spoke to me since the incident with the blind date she set me up on. She was a bit upset over that since it was a co-worker and it made things odd for her at her job. Even though I had apologized incessantly I never told her whom the man was that Ryan told her about. She was only over because she felt sorry for me for having an injury. This time I couldn't hold back. I told her everything. I told her how I met Troy and everything that had happened since. Lily was completely shocked. She scolded me for being so involved with a man I knew so little about. She warned me about rich men, that they are playboys and do what they please. I couldn't argue about that with her. So far she was right.

I needed a new life plan. What could I do to distract myself from my situation? On the one hand being with Troy had opened up a new door for me. I had never had these sorts of sexual experiences in my life. It was in new territory and it gave me the confidence in my body that I had never had before. I felt sexy. I felt like I could be naked and feel good about it. It was an intoxicating feeling. I thrived on it. I felt powerful. Since he revealed that I thought I was using him for sex, it made me feel powerful. But was he just manipulating me? I really couldn't tell. I knew so little about him, maybe this was just his way of turning things on me. But on the other hand I was feeling bonded to him. I had feelings for him. I was heart broken and jealous when I thought of him with another. It made me sick to my stomach. I was stuck between a rock and a hard place. I knew I needed to end it, but could I really do it? A day later, I had the answer.

My door buzzer rang. I answered, it was Troy, and I he was looking absolutely stunning. After having an inner battle with myself, I let him in. I was immediately aroused.

"Pack your bags," he said.

"What? Why?" I asked.

"I want to take you up the Hudson River, to my cottage up state."

"I can't. You're an awful person. I need to stay away from you." I said wringing my hands together.

"I do care for you Olivia. That's why I want to take you away. On my yacht, you will be the only woman. And at my cottage it will be just the two of us. There's nothing to worry about. I just want to go away with you. I do enjoy your company. Can we do this just this once? You can leave me forever after the trip and never look back, but right now, I need you."

His words hit me like a warm blanket that covered me and made me feel secure. It was everything I needed to hear from him. But this is what he did, he was a charmer, a manipulator, a womanizer, and I was falling for it. I stared at him, his large brown eyes silently pleaded with me. It was like he was two men combined into one. On one side he was the playboy sex god, and on the other he was the warm and comforting Troy that said the right things, ordered room service, and was cozy with me under the blankets. I loved one of them and loathed the other, but to experience the one I loved, I had to accept the one I hated.

"For how long?" I asked.

"Who cares? Let's escape this world and create our own." His delivery was sincere and I didn't doubt his genuine affection for me. I had to make a decision. Would I go and surely fall more deeply for this man? Or not go and began my movement forward in my life. A journey to focus on myself and forget about him, but live with the regret of not going and finding out what that adventure would hold. After all it wasn't everyday that a powerful rich man offered to take you up the Hudson on his private yacht. I had to choose, to have the experience or not too.

"When would we leave?" I asked.

"Now," he said.

"Now?" I said in shock. I can't just up and leave.

"Why not?" he asked.

"Well, because...because." I couldn't think of an excuse. My transfer at work was still in limbo and hadn't gone through, and I had not other affairs making me stay in New York. It had been two years since I had a vacation and honestly rushing around being late to everything had made me feel more stressed than ever. I did long to get away.

"Okay," I said. "Let me pack a few things."

He smiled that brilliant grin and I wanted to kiss him and slap him at the same time. Yes, he had won, but also he was glorious to look at.

Chapter 19

An hour later our car pulled up to Chelsea Piers on the Hudson. I had never been to this area of town. I really had no reason too. He escorted me down the pier to a beautiful old yacht. It was a refurbished 1920s style with shiny woods and polished silvers. It was beautiful.

"Alex will show you to our cabin and if you want you can join me on the decks for drinks and watch the coastline roll by. That's if you want to. If not, feel free to do whatever you like. But that's what I'll be doing."

"Okay thank you," I said as I followed the crewman inside the yacht down a long corridor and to our cabin. I gasped as I went in. An entire wall was tinted glass and looked straight out onto the water. There was a large plush bed, a master bathroom with a large soaking tub, and a walk in closet the size of my bedroom at home. Hanging in the closet were several dresses with the price tags still on as though they had just been bought for this trip. I found a flowing red one that fit me just perfectly. I freshened up brushing my long brown hair in the mirror. I applied extra coats of waterproof mascara around my large brown eyes, and put on a shade of a pouty pink on my full lips. I decided not to wear heels. More so because I was scared I would slip in them and fall overboard being lost in the river forever. Instead I put on the gold sandals that I had brought with me. They were delicate and laced all the way up my calf, just like a Roman Goddess. When I was finally done I joined Troy back on the deck. He was buried in his laptop doing some work I suppose.

"Olivia, you look stunning. Alex, will you bring us a late lunch please," Troy said as he stood up and grabbed my hand. He kissed it lightly and escorted me to a plush white bench. He poured some champagne and then said, "Here try this. It comes from my vineyard in France. I would like to know what you think."

I tasted the champagne. It was delicious, and I was thankful to have something to calm my nerves.

"It's delicious. Thank you for inviting me by the way."

"Thank you for coming. I see you found a dress that you like. It looks amazing on you."

"Thank you." I said wanting to continue my thanks with a "Why am I here, or a Why me?" follow up. But I didn't. Instead Troy locked eyes with me. He looked into my eyes, searching for something but I didn't know what. We stayed like this for so long, I took another drink of the champagne and got up to break the intensity. I stood up and walked along the deck. I looked out at the beauty of the city as we left the piers and headed up the Hudson.

The deck was very private and the pilots and crew never bothered us. We were left to our own devices. I had a sneaking suspicion that Troy had told the crew to leave us alone unless necessary. In a few seconds he was by my side looking out over the water with me.

"It's beautiful isn't it?"

"Sir, would you like lunch served here or in the dining room?" Alex asked.

Troy turned. "Here on the deck please Alex, and thank you. Could we have another bottle of champagne please?"

I had to say he was polite to his staff. I looked at him. Something was different. It felt like all those walls had come down. Was I fooling myself and seeing something that wasn't there? He grabbed my hand again and kissed it. Who was this man? I was used to the dominant sexual predator, but then I remembered the night we had room service and watch old movies. I had seen two sides to him. It was hard to keep up with who I would see next.

Alex came back and said, "Lunch is served."

"This way Olivia," Troy said. As he said it I realized how much I loved hearing him say my name.

The other side of the deck nearly knocked me on over with its splendor. There was a hot tub on the table with our delightful lunch laid out. Everything was white and pristine.

We took a bite of the steak and talked about its flavor and texture. We did this with everything we put in our mouths making a sort of game of it. It was a lot of fun and slowly my nervousness went away. The way Troy acted did not make me feel like less of person. He really acted like all this luxury and wealth wasn't his at all. As if he was excited and grateful to enjoy it and share it with me as well.

It was refreshing.

The yacht went lazily up the Hudson, and we were finally out of the urban areas. The scenery gave way to the Hudson Valley. There were tall trees of different varieties. The leaves were in the process of changing colors and it was a sea of gold, yellows, and oranges. It was absolutely stunning. I gasped at its beauty. We passed small farms and old barns. Every building was colonial, like the movie background of the Revolutionary War. I can't believe I had never ventured out of the city before to experience this. It was enchanting and tranquil. Now I knew why people left the city settle down out here. It was another world and it was relaxing. All the stress from my city life was melting away the further and further we went. The sound of the waves lapping at the side of the yacht was hypnotic, and I felt entranced. I could see myself wanting more and more of this in my life.

"What do you think?" Troy asked.

"I love it. I'm very happy. Thank you."

"I'm glad you like it," Troy said. "This is what I wanted to share with you. Most people don't leave Manhattan. They don't know that they are missing all this beauty. My cottage is surrounded by woods like these, and right now in autumn is the best time to visit."

"Where exactly are we going?" I asked.

"Just outside of Tarrytown. It's where my ancestors are from. Old, old family and traditions, and I think you will find it charming."

I smiled. This was the most romantic time I had ever had with him.

Troy laid down on the outdoor bed on the deck, and I knew what this was leading too. If I laid next to him, I was giving him permission to ravage me, in a sense. He looked up at me and bit his lower lip. I knew he wanted me, I wouldn't be here otherwise, but he was holding back. So I asked him, "What does that look mean?"

He laughed a little and said, "Come here. Come sit next to me."

I did as he asked. Once I was sitting next to him, Troy ran his hand down my back and said, "Olivia, I know this all must be strange for you, and I understand why. But that's precisely why I wanted you to come with me. You have that hesitation about being with me that most women don't have around me. That is extremely attractive to me. It shows that you value yourself, and that you can't be bought with money. I sense that from you, from the very moment I saw you. I wanted you from the moment I saw you, and I'm having a hard time containing myself now."

"I see," I said feeling a bit uncomfortable. I shifted in my seat.

Troy stopped rubbing my back and politely folded his hands together on top of his stomach. We were silent for a few minutes, while the water lapped at the side of the boat. Finally I broke the silence and said, "Maybe just a kiss, but keep your hands to yourself."

"I can do that," he said.

Because he was still lying down, I had to press my body against him to reach his mouth. I kissed him lightly. Then pulled my face a few inches away from him. We locked eyes. His lips were soft and I wanted more. I sighed a little at this thought. Then I leaned in and kissed him again, this time I allowed his tongue to explore my mouth. He moaned as he kissed me, and I relished the thought that I had this effect on him. I had this effect on a powerful rich man with just a kiss. I pulled away again and looked at him. I reached up and pushed his hair back away from his eyes and ran my hand down his face to his strong shoulders.

"It's complete torture that I'm not allowed to touch you. I want to touch your soft skin. I want it badly," he said with his hands still folded.

I giggled at the playful game we had going. It was fun and sensual. I played along,

"Well, maybe just with one hand."

Troy laughed and then placed one hand on my back and pulled me toward him. He kissed me passionately on the lips and then trailed kisses on my cheek and then down my neck to my cleavage. I moaned as he kissed the tops of my breast. His one hand rubbed down my back all the way down to my bottom. He squeezed and cupped it. I moaned with delight at his touch. I was getting more and more turned on and more wet. The fact that he was struggling to restrain himself really had my blood coursing through my body. I wanted him to touch me more. I wanted his fingers inside me. I moved myself around maneuvering myself on his hand. I moved over a few inches so that his hand moved from my bottom to my center. Once it was in place I rubbed myself against it, giving him permission to touch me there. I moaned and gasped as Troy put his hand in a cupped position on my center from behind. He was still keeping to his promise to use only one hand for now, and it made it that much more exciting.

I kissed him and put my hands against his chest. Troy pushed my panties aside and rubbed his hand against me. I was so wet; he slid two fingers inside of me with ease.

"Olivia, you feel like heaven."

I moaned at his words and at his fingers moving inside me. This was it, the point of no return. I couldn't stop if I wanted too. It felt too good and I wanted more. I grabbed his other hand from his chest and put it on my breast. I was giving him permission to explore my body. Troy was ecstatic and sat up quickly. This is what he had been longing for.

He removed his fingers from inside me and pulled the neckline of my dress down. He kissed my bare breasts and sucked on them. He groaned and licked and groaned and licked. He sighed with passion and his breathing was heavy. He looked at me and then unbuttoned his shirt and threw it off. I stared at his magnificent body. He was well toned and I couldn't help myself so I kissed his chest up and down. Troy arched himself up toward me. He ran his hands through my hair and all over my body. Next he got on his knees at the edge of the bed and kissed my legs. He flung my skirt up to my waist and climbed on top of me. He rubbed his body against mine. I wanted him, and I wanted him now. I reached down and peeled my panties off. Troy moaned at the sight of me. He unzipped his pants and took them off. Then he put the tip of his rock hard shaft inside me, and slowly pushed it in. I cried out in ecstasy. It was hard, long, and wide and it filled every inch of me. I wrapped my hands around his neck to steady myself. He put his hands under my bottom and controlled the rhythm of us back and forth. After a few minutes like this he pulled out of me and pulled my dress off.

Now we were completely naked and on top of each other. We explored each other's bodies. Troy sat on the bench and I straddled him in a backward cowgirl position. He put his hands on my hips and bounced me up and down on top of him. He moved his hands from my waist up to my breasts and massaged them. Then he moved them back down to my waist to control the movement. He slammed my body against his over and over.

In this position, we both came. I relaxed a little as I enjoyed my orgasm. I couldn't believe I was having wild sex aboard his million-dollar yacht. For some reason though, it felt right. I deserved some adventure.

Chapter 20

We fell asleep with a cozy blanket on top of us. I don't know how many hours had passed when I woke up.

"Olivia," Troy said as I opened my eyes.

I had almost forgot where I was. I popped up and looked around. I was on the deck of the yacht. I stretched and wrapped the blanket around me

"Did you sleep well?" Troy asked.

"Sort of,"

"Come on, let's get you into a warm bed. It's chilly out here." He led me to my cabin and we crawled into the warm bed and went back to sleep. It was very comforting and the heat from his body kept me warm.

I was going to Troy's country home, not just a random apartment. This was his real home, in upstate New York. Something about that felt comforting and cozy.

The boat was skirting the coastline for an hour. We began to pull into the old docks of Tarrytown. We finally docked and disembarked. I picked up my long skirt and stepped of the boat onto the dock. It was good to be on solid ground again.

There was a black SUV waiting for us. We got in the car and headed out of town. We passed old houses and cobblestone streets. It was as if we had gone back in time. I could almost imagine women in giant ball gowns and horse drawn carriages. There were light posts that had rarely changed in a hundred years except going from gas to electricity. In front of most of the houses there were one or two steps built into the sidewalk. This is where carriages pulled up to let people out. It was enchanting. Almost nothing had changed. I looked at Troy and thought how lucky he was to be brought up in such an environment. I kissed him on the cheek. He looked at me and gave me a squeeze. But something was plaguing me, it was the fact that I still really didn't know this man.

We finally arrived on an empty dirt road that ran down a vast forest of tall trees.

My breath was taken away. In front of use were rows of trees on either side of the lane covered for a mile at least, and at the end of it was large mansion.

"Is that the cottage?" I asked.

"Yes," he answered.

Clearly we had different ideas of what a cottage was. This was a vast sprawling house in the forest. It was old and beautiful.

We pulled up to the house and I got out of the car and stared up at it. It was done in the Colonial style.

"Do you like it?" Troy asked.

"Yes, it looks peaceful."

"Good. Let's put our things away and go for a hike. If you would like?"

"Yes, that sounds perfect."

I put my bags away in the master bedroom and met him outside.

We walked hand in hand to the trailhead and it felt good to do something so normal with him. I looked around at the beauty of this place. The trees were massive and towered high into the sky. Troy stopped and looked around, he was really present in this place. He looked at me and said,

"This is my favorite place. I've been coming here to hike since I was a kid. It has everything. It's a perfect playground for a child. There are vast stretches of meadow. You can find thick green forest and small wetland stream areas. If you climb higher you would reach cliffs that drop off into a canyon and the view is stunning."

I took in a deep breath and forgot all about everything that plagued me in life.

I put my hands over my head and stretched long and reached high over me. I bent over at the waist touching the ground and stretching the back of my legs. It felt good to warm my muscles.

"Let's go down to the canyon. This way," he said as he veered off to the right.

He quickened his pace, clearly wanting to take the lead and walk ahead of me. I let him. It felt good to be guided and led somewhere. He wanted to share this place with me, for whatever reason. I felt good about that. I watched him from behind. His reflexes were cat like as we crawled over obstacles and jumped over puddles. It was impressive, and I was enjoying watching him. I was really looking at him like a piece of meat.

Something told me he wouldn't mind.

Chapter 21

We hiked in silence. Each of us was in our own world observing nature, and our gorgeous surroundings.

I loved nature and being here was therapeutic for me. Being around plant life and the wild made me feel like a primitive creature again. There was beauty in that. All the stresses of our daily American lives stripped away, and you could imagine yourself as a basic creature in the wild. Hunting and gathering the food the Earth created for us, sleeping under the stars, and bathing in a stream, were all the basics of living, or used to be anyway.

It was sensual in strange way, when you really thought about it. I was looking down at my feet watching my every step lost in this thought, when I collided with Troy. I didn't even realize he had stopped in front of me. He must have had his back to me, because he didn't even see me coming. We toppled over and landed on the ground. I landed on top of him.

"Whoa, calm down. I surrender," he playfully called. Why was this guy able to turn me into a bumbling buffoon? First it was the coffee incident when we first met, and now this. I was literally always falling for him.

"Sorry, I wasn't watching...oh never mind." I laughed at the situation. He laughed too then picked me up off of him and said, "Let's keep going," he continued on down the trail. I heard him laughing and enjoying himself. It made my heart sing. He was so darn adorable. We hiked for another half hour. He was once again ahead of me. He came to the edge of a dry creek bed.

"Let's go this way."

"Off the trail? That's not a good idea. That's how you get lost out here," I said suddenly feeling like a mother once I said it. He looked at me and grinned and started down the creek bed.

"We won't go far. Just find a spot to take a little break."

I followed him down the dry creek bed. There was a small bend and it dipped even deeper. This created an area that was completely private from the trail. I suddenly felt nervous and jittery, like a child that was playing hide and seek. He stopped and sat against a moss-covered boulder. The area was lush and green and looked like a fairy would appear at any second. The leaves hung low from the trees, and the round rocks had been smoothly shaped by the running water that appeared in the rainy season.

"Come take a break," he said as he padded the empty space on the rock next to him. I sat next to him.

"It's beautiful, isn't it?" he said looking around. Then he looked over at me and continued, "Just like you."

I turned my face toward him to tell him something but there was no time. As soon as I turned my head, he planted a kiss on me.

He put his arm on my lower back and rubbed it up and down. It was a comforting feeling. Then he slid his hand down to my buttocks and squeezed them. I moaned in response. I wanted him.

He moved his other hand on my chests and massaged my breasts. My nipples immediately went hard. We kissed and touched in the wild of the forest. I ran my hand against his chest and went further to his hard shaft. It was rock hard through his pants. I rubbed it up and down. He moaned and pulled away from me. He stood up and grabbed my hands and brought me to my feet. He turned me around and pushed me over. I placed my hands on the boulder we were once sitting on. He pushed my feet apart with his foot and then peeled off my spandex hiking pants down to my ankles. This was exactly what we had done once in his bedroom. I could remember that like it was yesterday. He liked this position. He moved around and hand his hard cock in his hand and placed the tip inside me.

This was happening, my first outdoor sexual experience. I was astonished that I had never done this before. Though, Central Park wasn't exactly a private place. However, I never really had the pleasure of enjoying the outdoors with a sexy vibrant man, who would have sex anywhere.

He put his hands on my back then pushed himself deep inside me. I yelled out and called out his name, "Troy, Troy, I want you." His hands cupped my breast and then he reached up and pulled on my ponytail gently. He tugged on it and my head went back in response to it. I let out a soft moan and looked up at the environment. The wild abandon of it all was exciting. " Harder, harder," I breathlessly said.

He pounded me and slammed harder. I looked around me, at the trees and all the beauty of nature. Us being in the wild having sex like primitive man and woman. With that thought I climbed higher and higher, and then I released into climax.

I steadied myself on the boulder. My orgasm was intense. Troy pulled out of me and turned me toward him. He locked eyes on mine. He was so in the moment it drove me crazy. He picked me up and propped me on the boulder. He leaned down and gave one long quick lick.

"I love the taste of you," he said. I sighed in enjoyment. He knew all the right things to say. He pushed himself between my thighs and entered me again. He reached around and cupped my buttocks in his hands and went hard and fast. He buried his face in my neck and released himself inside of me.

Chapter 22

We hiked up back out of the canyon in silence. I had the biggest smile on my face. I was really having fun out here. It made a huge difference to get away from everything.

I didn't have to worry about another woman out here. It was what pure security felt like. It was such a drastic change from my normal insecure being. I was in such a relaxed state it made me truly happy.

The next day we slept in late. I was starting to feel restless so I got out of bed and went to find coffee. Troy stayed asleep. I looked at him and covered him with a blanket. In the kitchen I made coffee and filled my mug. I stared down and laughed at the liquid. Coffee, it's how this all started. Thank you coffee, I thought to myself. I roamed around the house and decided I would find a book to curl up with. It was a nice autumn grey morning and it made me want to snuggle up with a good book. I found the library and moved my hands over the bookshelves. There were so many to choose from. There were a few books piled on the desk so I went to inspect those. I was not expecting what I saw. There were framed pictures of his parents and siblings. Troy suddenly felt very human to me. He was a real man with a real family that he cared about. This was becoming more complicated. The longer I stayed here the more I would fall for him, the real him. Not the dirty talking man I thought he was.

I went upstairs and woke him up. He grabbed me and pulled me into bed and began kissing me. He started with the talk, "I want to put my cock inside you. Do you want my cock inside you?"

I was aroused, I needed him to stop, but it was always so hard. His voice was like a dream and it was hypnotic when he talked to me like that. I finally wrestled my way free and stood up away from the bed.

"What's the matter?" he asked with a confused look on his face. "Are you all right?"

"No, I'm not. I think I should go back to the city."

"Why?"

"It's hard to explain but I... feel like I'm suffocating here."

That was the wrong thing to say. The look that came over his face was one of anger and disappointment. "What do you want Olivia? Tell me because I can't figure it out."

"I don't know," and that was the honest truth. I really didn't know what I wanted. Just then there was a loud bang outside. We both stood in shock and went to the window. The grey sky had turned into an all out storm. What we heard was thunder. Flashes of lightning lit the sky. Then the lights went out. It was clear that I wasn't going anywhere. Troy looked at me and grinned, I sighed and rolled my eyes in response. Once again I was his prisoner.

The late morning gave way to evening faster than usual, or so I thought. Turns out that the sky was just that dark from the storm. It raged outside and it scared me a little. I wasn't used to being out in the country in a storm. It was thrilling, but also made me feel frightened. Troy built a fire in the parlor and we sat on the rug in front of it surrounded by pillows. We lit candles for light, but it set a romantic mood. Troy once again went into action taking care of me. He made us cold sandwiches and coffee and made sure I was comfortable. Just the sort of things that made me go back and forth emotionally between loving him and wanting to escape him. It was an emotional roller coaster.

"Look if you still want to leave tomorrow I will drive you myself, but for now we are stuck here so can we just have a little fun. Lighten the mood some? I can tell that you are overthinking right now," he said looking at me.

That was surprising, maybe this man could read me better than he let on. He was right, I was overthinking. It would feel better to just be present in the moment.

"I have an idea," he said. He grabbed a candle and walked out of the room. I had no idea what he was up to. But I'm sure it was something extraordinary, he was in fact an extraordinary man. He came back in a few minutes later with a book. He started reading aloud to me. I was in shock. Not only was it intoxicating to have a man read aloud to me, but he picked the perfect book for a stormy day in upstate New York in the Hudson Valley. It was Washington Irving's Sleepy Hollow. I covered myself up with a thick blanket and listened intently. That was it. I was hooked. I wanted this man now and for the rest of my life. Then I remembered how quickly he was to cast me aside and tried to be with Amber.

That thought made my stomach turn. I could never trust him.

Chapter 23

I cast those thoughts of uncertainty aside and once again forced myself to be in the moment. I needed to enjoy myself.

Like Troy said, I was overthinking everything and all that did was stress me out. Fortunately the blackout provided a good distraction. It was fun having to do everything by candlelight. We spent the night taking turns reading aloud and laughing. We played cards and other board games, and eventually we ended up exhausting ourselves in front of the fire. It was magical and it felt surreal. Was this really my life right now? I thought to myself.

He propped himself up on his elbow and looked at me. His hand caressed my face and brushed through my hair. His hand trailed down my neck and over my chest, down my belly and over my thighs. His touch was searing hot to my skin. He had this affect on me. I was already wet and aroused. My nipples were at attention, pert, and hard. He put one in his mouth. He kissed it slowly and licked around it. It was sensual and romantic. This was the first time we slowly enjoyed each other's bodies instead of partaking in a sexual game. Troy's mouth covered mine and he kissed me deeply. I ran my hands down his body and rubbed down his back. Then I pulled him close to me and hugged him tightly. I wrapped my legs around his body in a full body hug. He moaned in response to my needing him. I locked eyes with him. He looked down at me and smiled. I responded with a smile. He buried his head in my neck and that's how we fell asleep. Intertwined, naked, and not having sex. It was invigorating and confusing.

The next day the weather had cleared, and I decided to stay. I went back and forth thinking I should leave and then my heart would tell me to stay. I stopped fighting it and stayed. We went for another hike in the freshly rained on trails. The air smelled of wet ground and rain and it was beautiful.

We hiked again into the wilderness. This time we went up. We climbed higher and higher until the trail ended at a gorgeous over look. You could see for miles from up there. Troy began to yell, "Hello!" and listening back as it echoed from the canyon below. It was adorable.

"Join me," he said. I started to yell with him and we laughed at hearing our own voices echo back at us. After a few minutes of laughing, drinking some water, and resting, Troy stood before me. He grabbed my hand and rubbed it on his hard rod. How was he already hard? I thought. We hadn't even had any real contact yet.

He guided my hand over it, just the way he wanted to be touched. Then he unzipped his pants and pulled it out. I forgot how big it was, and again my eyes widened. I played with it. Really examined it. The smooth pink skin was perfect. Then, there on the ledge of this massive over look, I knelt down in front of him and put the tip in my mouth. Troy moaned and tilted his head back. I used my hand to tug back and forth on the base of it. It was so large, there was no way the entire thing would fit in my mouth. Still, I enjoyed having it in my mouth.

I looked up at him as I sucked on the tip. He moaned as he looked down at me, then he smiled that brilliant grin. He touched my face softly with his hand and ran his hand in my hair. I took the tip out of my mouth and licked it up and down like a popsicle. I did this for a few minutes, and then Troy pulled away from me.

He came down to the ground with me and laid me down on the ground. He unlaced my boots and took them off. Then he peeled my pants down. Now the bottom half of me was naked. He got on top and pressed himself down on me. His soft smooth skin rubbed against mine. It felt delicious. He kissed me on the mouth. Then stared down at me and asked, "Do you want me inside you?"

"Yes."

"Why?"

"Because it feels good. I want to have you inside me, because it feels good."

He grinned. He loved hearing me say that. He reached down and took his big shaft in his hand and put it inside me. He slowly slid inside me, inch by inch. Just when I thought it was all inside me, there was more. He was good at the art of prolonging. Increasing my anticipation. Finally, he was all inside me. He was deep within me. He moaned loudly and pulled his head up looking around. Then he looked at me again and said, "Look around Olivia. Look where we are. We are lucky to have found each other. Two people that enjoy nature, look at it."

I did as he commanded. I looked around and he looked around. He started to move in and out of me, but neither of us looked at each other. We looked at our surroundings as we fucked, bringing each other to pure ecstasy. First, he went slow and then pounded me. I put my legs up in the air and then wrapped them around his body. I wanted him completely inside me. Then Troy stopped and pulled out of me completely. I was confused. I knew he hadn't come yet. He pushed himself down the length of my body. He put his hand on my center and parted me with his fingers. He moaned with delight and said, "beautiful."

He did that for a while. Looking at me and fondling me, completely enjoying what he saw. It made me feel very sexy and I was thrilled with each sigh that escaped his mouth. Then he put his mouth on me. First trailing light kisses all around and then using his tongue to penetrate me. I arched my back in response. It felt like I was melting into the ground. He used his tongue to apply pressure and move left to right. That was all I needed. I came almost immediately into his mouth. He eagerly drank it up.

After watching me writhe around in full orgasm he climbed back on top of me. He pushed my thighs open wide with his hands and then guided his shaft back inside me. He pushed deep in, fucking me again. He went faster and faster until he yelled out in ecstasy. He collapsed on top of me. All of his weight was on me and I could smell the intoxicating odor of his skin. I licked his shoulder. I was surprised at myself. I no longer went through the process of questioning everything. I was just driven by pure lust. It felt good. It felt primitive.

Like we were a couple of animals in the wild.

Chapter 24

We spent most of the day up on that ledge. It was a good place and I never wanted to leave. He finally persuaded me to hike back down to the house. I thought about my life in New York and how I would eventually need to get back. This was a nice vacation, but eventually I needed to get back to reality.

Later that night we had dinner and watched a movie. Then the phone rang. It was strange because that phone had not made any noise the entire time we had been there. Troy answered, then he was quiet and looked at me. I was confused. He took the phone in the other room making me even more suspicious. Then he came back in.

"What is it?" I asked.

"We're going to have company tomorrow," he said, his face impassive.

"Company? Who?"

"My family."

The next day, his mother was waiting for us in the parlor downstairs. Troy came up to tell me she had arrived.

"I'll meet you downstairs."

"Meet me? You're not going to wait for me?" I yelled out in disbelief.

I couldn't meet his mother. I was merely a sex toy, I was not about to feel uncomfortable in front of his family.

"I'm already dressed and if I have to sit here watching you brush your long locks while you're naked, we will never leave this room. Besides, you take forever to get dressed so I might as well go down and keep our guest occupied before she comes up here herself and knocks on the door. Hell, she won't even knock she'll just burst right in."

He laughed when I froze in mid brush stroke. "Okay, maybe you should go down. I'll join you in a bit."

Troy came over and kissed me on top of my head. "You are a beautiful woman."

I smiled at him. He turned and winked at me as he closed the door behind him. What had I gotten myself into? This was a whirlwind.

I went into fast track mode getting dressed and prepped as fast I could. I didn't want to take too much time. And I didn't want to go down looking like a mess.

I pulled my long hair into a high slick pony tale on top of my head with simple earrings on my ears. I put on a conservative but elegant day dress that went well passed my knees. I wore kitten heels in white and nude stockings. There, I thought. I looked just as elegant and formal as any woman could. Not a complete slut who fucked this woman's son every chance I got. I took one last look in the mirror and breathed in deep. I could do this. This was all make-believe anyhow, or so it seemed. This was just another part of the crazy things that had happened to me since I met Troy.

A few minutes later I walked into the parlor. Troy was sitting on the windowsill of a large bay window smoking a cigar. Across from him in a winged back chair was a fiery little red head.

"Oh hello, you must be Olivia. It's so good to meet you." She ran over to me like a child and gave me a big warm hug.

I was immediately confused. I was expecting an icy hello and judgmental look. This was not at all what I was getting from her. In fact it was quite the opposite. I picked my arms up and hugged her back and looked at Troy who was all smiles. What the hell was going on here?

"How are you liking the cottage and the country? It must be such a change from the city for you. My that is a lovely dress, but

I was hoping you would join me on a ride. It's been a few weeks since I've been here and I miss those little horses dearly. Would you mind changing and joining me?"

    I stood in amazement not knowing which of the whirlwind of questions to answer first. I looked at her and realized she was wearing a riding outfit of spandex black pants and riding boots. I looked at Troy for some sort of sign of what I should do. He smiled at me and then snubbed his nose in the air as though he had no idea that she had asked me a question. I completely forgot that there were horses on the property. They were located far from the house and were taken care of by a caretaker. I narrowed my eyes at Troy a bit and then finally answered the eager woman at my side. "Sure I would love to go riding with you. I'll go up and change and be down in a few minutes."

    "Excellent! I'll be down here with Troy. Don't take too long now you hear?"

    "Okay, I'll be back soon." I left the room in complete confusion. Well, she wasn't the ice queen I thought she would be. She was all kindness and warm hospitality. I laughed a little as I thought that life will never be boring with him as he always keeps me on my toes.

Chapter 25

Ten minutes later I was walking down the stairs back to join our guest. Troy and his mother stood in the foyer waiting for me.

"There she is."

I gave Troy a wide-eyed look in response. Again he just smiled at me.

She and I headed out the door and Troy gave me a quick peck on the cheek. She watched every second of our goodbye exchange.

We walked to the stables and talked. Or I should say she talked. She asked many questions, but never paused for me to answer. Soon, I thought getting through this would be no problem at all because all I had to do was listen. That was easy enough.

We entered the stables and there stood Mr. Grace, the foreman.

"Oh, Mr. Grace, how nice to see you. Would you saddle two horses for me and Olivia to ride please."

"Yes, ma'am. Good day to you both."

She watched my face with a hawk's eyes. I think she was waiting for some sort of reaction. Was she testing me?

"Actually, Mr. Grace could you join us on our ride if it's not too much trouble. I would like to hear more about the business and upkeep of the stables."

"Yes, ma'am it would be my pleasure."

We set out on our ride. It was a pleasant day and Troy's mother, or Tabitha, as she told me to call her, did most of the talking. She kept an eye out on me though the entire time. It was unnerving, but it gave me hope. She was going through all this trouble to check me out, which meant Troy might have told her more about me. That was a thrilling thought. A confusing thought, but thrilling.

After the ride we sat down to brunch. Troy had mysteriously disappeared and left a note that he was seeing to business. I sincerely doubted that, and he just was enjoying putting this torture on me. The conversation continued and was all politeness.

"And of course you must come to my niece, Jessica's wedding this weekend. I'm sure Troy told you all about it? I wasn't sure if you already had a dress, but if not do not worry, dear. I know the best store in town and they can deliver some to you tomorrow."

"The wedding? Oh yes, of course. Getting a dress is on my to do list." I covered up my confusion. Troy had not mentioned a wedding. I assumed his entire family would be there. I was already nervous.

"Listen dear, I must confess to you."

Oh no, here it comes, I thought. What now, is she going to tell me that I needed to leave Troy and never to come back again? Of course a woman like her doesn't want her son marrying a nobody that worked a day job at a spa.

"I came to meet you on purpose. When I heard Troy had brought a girl home, I knew it must be serious. He hardly does that. It is rare." She paused. "I love my son and don't want to see him make a mistake. You seem all right though."

"Okay...um, thank you." I was so confused. What was she talking about? This was a weird conversation.

Finally brunch was over and Tabitha left and gave me a big hug. It was all very confusing.

Chapter 26

This wasn't an ordinary wedding. It was an extravaganza.

I knew it would be classy and romantic, but what I didn't expect was to experience the extreme sexual confidence of one of Troy's brother, Will. Nor did I expect to discover that Troy actually was promised to another woman.

The ceremony was beautiful, well what I could remember, since I was so nervous to be around Troy's family. The reception was a grand party. It felt like a ball out of an old Civil War film. I was talking to his cousin, Katherine, when I noticed a woman flirting with Troy. It was very obvious, so much so that I was embarrassed that he wasn't stopping her, knowing well that I had been introduced to his family as his girlfriend.

"Who is that woman with Troy?"

Kathleen looked in the direction I motioned to. "Oh that's Susannah. She's madly in love with him."

"Really."

"Yes, Susannah and Troy were promised to each other since they were babies in an unofficial way. It's an old tradition really, that we don't practice much anymore. But at the time it was very real for their parents. Somehow Troy talked his way out of it. Broke that girl's poor heart. But that was a couple of years ago, so I wouldn't worry your pretty little head about it."

The reception went on later and later. I drank a lot of champagne and had a good time. Troy spent most of the time catching up with friends and family as he had been away for months. I had danced several dances with a few of the gorgeous men young and old. But Troy's brother, Will never asked me to dance. I thought that was strange. He seemed mysterious yet charming at the same time, but something about the way he looked at me sent shivers up my spine. It was the same look Troy gave me in bed. Trouble, I thought.

I locked eyes with him a few times, which was irritating, as I didn't want to encourage him. However, I assumed he was locking eyes with all the girls that drooled over him in that reception hall. That was until I went into the coat closet to grab my coat. I walked into the coatroom to grab my brown fur, as I was about to go outside and get some fresh air and distance. I needed an escape. I went into the coatroom and took my heels off. My feet were done from the entire day of standing on them, followed by dancing. I dangled my shoes in one hand and was searching through the coats with the other, when I heard a deep voice say, "You're Olivia."

I turned to see a tall man standing there, staring at me. His eyes lingered on my body trailing his gaze from my feet up to my face. It was Will, and he had a dangerous dark look about him. It took me a few seconds to answer because his presence stunned me. I finally said, "I am."

After I answered he moved in closer, and I instantly took a few steps back. Suddenly I was as far back as I could go, amongst all the other coats. He put only a few inches between us and looked down at me. His large green eyes locked with mine. He pushed the hair out of my face and trailed his hand down my cheek and said, "I saw you watching me tonight. I was watching you, watching me. Did you like what you saw?"

My eyes widened and my mouth opened a little. I had not expected him to be so forward, but of course he would be this confident. What didn't he have to be confident about? I thought. I finally just shook my head no, in response to his question.

The back of his hand went down my face, down my neck and onto my heaving cleavage. I couldn't believe it; he was touching the top of my breasts. This man was Troy's brother!

What was worse was that I didn't stop him. I looked down at his hand on my breasts and then looked up at him with lust in my eyes. He just grinned at me; he knew what he was doing. Then I heard a female voice say, "Olivia?"

I quickly stepped away from him and came out of the coatroom to find Troy's mother, Tabitha looking for me. Perfect.

I couldn't let her see me with Will, alone though. "I'm right here."

She looked at me, and the coat in my hand. "You're not leaving, are you?"

"Oh no," I turned to look back at the coatroom. No sign of Will. I was relieved. "I was just going to grab some air outside."

"Well that will have to wait," she reached out her hand, "Jessica's about to throw the bouquet. Come on!"

I grabbed her hand and let her lead me back into the main room, but not before looking over my shoulder to see Will leaning against the door smirking at me.

I was feeling completely perplexed at my behavior with Will. Why couldn't I stop myself? Yes, he resembled Troy greatly, but was rougher around the edges, less refined somehow and bigger. In more ways than one? I wondered idly. But more to the point he was his brother! He was confident, demanding, and I suspected he knew how to please a woman just like his brother.

No, I reminded myself. I was with Troy, in love with Troy.

I needed to stop thinking about his brother.

Chapter 27

An hour later I was walking down the hallway of the reception looking for Troy, with enough champagne in me to make me almost forget what had happened in the coatroom, when I heard: "Are you looking for me?"

Will stood there looking at me with that cocky grin. I froze for a few seconds. Then I did something I wasn't expecting. Maybe it was the champagne. Whatever the reason, I played along.

"Do you think I would be looking for you? I'm looking for Troy. Your brother, or did you forget that he was your brother?" I said coquettishly, as I put my hands on my curvy hips.

Will walked over to me like he had before, putting only a few inches between our bodies. I looked up at him and he looked down at me and down my dress.

He leaned in close to me, his breath caressing my ear as he said, "I know you want to fuck me. I know you want me inside you."

I gasped. I was not expecting him to talk to me like that. It was intoxicating and it reminded me of Troy that day when we first met. What was wrong with me? I wanted this and it was so wrong, then he continued, "And if you pass up this opportunity, we may never have another like it."

Then he paused and locked eyes with me, his green eyes looking down at me and continued, "You know it's true, Olivia."

He moved his mouth across my lips, brushing them lightly. His mouth was soft and I could smell the whiskey on his breath. My hands had a mind of their own as they reached up and touched his chest. He must have seen this as an encouragement because he put his hand on the small of my back and pulled me against him. I could feel his hard member on me and it was huge. It made me instantly aroused to know that he was already hard. I gasped at his aggressive move.

"I'm going to lick you until you cry. You know you want it. You want me to taste you, fuck you, make you scream my name."

Hearing him say things like that made me wet. I was feeling aroused but confused. I wanted to run away and at the same time I did want to fuck him. The very thought of this brutish man inside me made my head began to spin and I realized I was drunker than I thought I was.

He moved his hand down from the small of my back to my bottom and to the hem of my dress. He kept going until his hand was resting on the back of my bare thigh. His thumb was under my dress and rubbed lightly against the crease between my thigh and cheek. The anticipation was building inside me. This was dangerous. I needed him to stop. I needed him to stop now.

Will covered my mouth with his and parted my lips with his tongue. His kiss was deep and passionate and his breathing was growing heavy.

"Do you want me in your mouth? Slide myself in and out?" he asked between kisses. I couldn't open my eyes and my voice was barely a whisper as I simply said, "Yes."

I forgot that we were still in the hallway, a public place as he moved his hand from the back of my thigh to the front of my thigh. I gasped again at the proximity of his hand to my center. Then I pulled away completely and took a few steps back. I remembered whom I was and that I was with Troy.

"No please stop, get away from me."

Will looked at me and grinned with a confident smirk. I hated letting him have that power over me, but I couldn't stop it. I was hypnotized by lust for this man. I needed to snap out of it.

"Don't touch me again."

Will slowly took a few steps forward. Just then Troy came out of nowhere. I don't know how long he had been there or what he had heard or seen, but he was on us so fast he was a blur.

Bam. He punched Will in the jaw.

Will stumbled back a few steps. Then he came back and punched Troy in the stomach. I screamed, "No. Leave him alone please!"

Troy doubled over grabbing his waist with his arms. It only took him a second to catch his breath and from his bent over position came up with a punch under Will's jaw. Will went sailing back in the air flat on his back.

I was stunned. Troy yelled at him. "Leave her out of this. Don't you dare touch her."

He turned and grabbed my hand and led me away. He was fuming with anger. Even in my drunken state I thought this is it, I've lost him.

Stupid girl.

Chapter 28

We rode in silence back to his house. I knew he would want nothing to do with me.

We entered the foyer and Troy grabbed me and then kissed me aggressively.

"Don't ever do that again." He commanded. "You're mine. Do you understand that? Mine and only mine."

I nodded in dismay. I was scared but elated to hear that he still wanted me, and more so that I was his. I wanted to feel like his property. It felt good. This newfound extreme jealousy turned out to be a good thing. It put the fire back in our sexual escapades. Troy scooped me up in his strong arms and carried me up the stairs to our bedroom. He threw me on the bed and turned on all the lights. I was confused by what was going on.

"You have to pay for what you did tonight."

I opened my eyes wide. I was not sure what he meant by that.

"What do you want me to do?" I asked.

"Stand up and strip," he said angrily.

I was helpless. I got off the bed and walked over to him. I stood only a few inches from him and took off all my clothes. I stripped completely nude. I stood there with my hands crossed in front of me. I wanted him to feel the urge to reach out and touch me. I took a few steps backwards to add to the tease.

"Get on all fours," he said. My eyes opened wide. I was not expecting him to say that.

"What?" I asked in a whisper. He repeated again, but slower and angrier.

"I said, get, on, all, fours." There was a moment of silence then he continued, "Now. Get on your knees. You tease. You slut."

I was being punished and I liked it. It was clear I had hurt him. I don't know what was going on between him and his brother, but I had come into an already existing feud. I had never seen Troy angry before, and I was ashamed to know that I was aroused and excited by it.

I realized that what he had said before about me was true. I did want him for sex, this is the way I liked being treated by him. This is when I responded to him the most. This is who I had become. Had I always had this rampant sexual side to me? Did he just bring it out in me? I could feel myself changing. I didn't know who I was anymore. He ignited my addiction for this type of treatment from our very first meeting and I haven't been able to get away from it since he started it. It wasn't just Troy that I had become addicted to, it was being dominated and treated this way in the bedroom.

That was a sobering revelation.

I got on all fours and looked up at him.

"Crawl to my bed," he said. His lips were set in a hard line. I started crawling.

"Slower," he yelled. I flinched at the volume of his voice. Then I went slower.

"Did you want to fuck my brother? Did you want his cock inside you?"

I stopped and looked at him. My eyes watered over a bit.

"Tell me!" he yelled.

I narrowed my eyes, and said, "Yes." It was the truth. In the moment Will had me aroused and I wanted to know what he would feel like inside me. Troy wanted to play this game, and I was going to do my part. He wanted to punish me and I would give him more to punish me over.

Chapter 29

The length of his stride doubled and he came over to me. He picked me up and threw me on the bed. "Did you want his cock in your mouth?"

"Yes," I answered. He was silent and motionless. I continued, "I wanted to slide his cock in my mouth. I wanted to suck on it."

He angrily unzipped his pants and climbed on top of me. He pushed himself between my thighs. He put his finger inside me and said, "You are wet. Is that for me or my brother?"

I realized he was expecting to feel that I was wet, it was what validated him and encouraged him. I nodded my head yes.

"Say it. Say he made you wet," he said.

I paused with my eyes wide until he commanded again, "Say it!"

I did as he commanded, "Your brother, Will. He made me wet, so wet."

His eyes narrowed, "Do you want him over me?"

"No."

"Yes, you do. I saw you."

"I'm drunk and ... confused."

"Lies."

I looked at him and wasn't sure if this was a game anymore. It was escalating. I was scared and aroused at the same time. I finally said, "He accosted me in the hallway. I would never ... I tried to get away."

Troy looked away from me. I could see the pain in his eyes. I wanted to console him and apologize and tell him he's the only one for me. But I knew he needed this, he wanted to demean me into obedience and I was going to let him.

What's worse was that I was enjoying this. I wanted this.

"This is mine. Do you understand me? No one else touches this."

I looked at him and nodded my head yes. He was being commanding and dominant, yet I knew it was coming from a place of jealousy and it turned me on beyond anything I had ever experienced. This powerful man was having his heart broken by me. He didn't like it. I liked knowing I had that effect on him, as much as it made me feel guilty, it made me feel desirable. I was getting my fix. This was what I had become addicted to.

Troy grabbed me roughly. He reached down and grabbed his cock and shoved it inside me hard.

I spread my legs apart wider. I needed it, and I needed it rough. I grabbed the back of his thighs with my hands and pulled them toward me.

He went deep inside of me. He moved faster and faster, slamming his body against mine. He looked down at me, straight into my eyes. There it was again, the pain and hurt in his eyes. He placed his hand on my face and closed his eyes as though he couldn't stand to look at me. He groaned, but it wasn't one of ecstasy it was of anger. I moaned louder. This felt so good. I was so wet, he slid in and out of me with ease. I was enjoying this, I think this only made him angrier. He didn't want me to enjoy this.

He pulled out of me and flipped me over. I was on all fours again on top of the bed. He grabbed my hips. He entered me from behind and slammed hard against me. He pulled my hair. He pulled it hard and slammed me, pounded me hard. I was so aroused by this that I immediately climaxed. I yelled out in ecstasy. I breathed hard. I wanted this more and more. Troy put all his weight on my back and I laid down on my stomach. He continued pumping away at me from behind. I buried my head in the pillow. He moved in and out of me hard and fast. He was sweating and breathing heavily. Finally he released himself. I didn't want it to end. I wanted more of the roughness and the anger.

He collapsed on top of me. We stayed like that in silence. He reached out and grabbed my hand and squeezed it. I wasn't sure what that meant. Was it affection or was it possession? Finally he pushed himself up pulled out of me. He rolled me onto my back and looked at me. His eyes narrowed. He was still angry. He got off the bed and grabbed his pants off the floor. He put them on while staring at me with a fire in his eyes.

Then he left the room.

Chapter 30

The next morning, I woke up alone in bed. I immediately remembered that I was being punished. In the light of day it didn't feel good. The punishment games we had played the night before were erotic then, but now it felt wrong.

My head ached from drinking too much, and I felt light headed as I stood up. That had to be true. I knew we could get over this. There was too much passion between us. We were a fire that burned bright and anything that came between us only made that fire burn hotter.

I went downstairs to the kitchen, but Troy was not down yet. He must still be asleep I thought. I made coffee and breakfast and decided I would take him breakfast in bed as a peace offering. I made omelets and pancakes and arranged them just so on the silver treys. I carried the trey upstairs to the spare bedroom. I knocked on the door. There was no answer. I turned the doorknob and it opened. I carried the trey in, but the room was empty. I felt foolish.

I walked outside and looked around. It was a beautiful sunny autumn day and it was crystal clear. No fog in sight. The stables off in the far distance caught my attention. Of course! I thought to myself, the stables. I set off in that direction. I didn't see Troy, but I did see the foreman.

"Hello, ma'am," Mr. Grace the foreman said.

"Hello, I was looking for Troy, have you seen him?" I asked.

He hesitated. He looked at me, and quickly looked away. What was he hiding? What did he know? Then he answered, "Yes, he went out for a ride this morning, with Susannah."

I cringed at the words. The woman he was originally promised to. The woman who was all over him at the wedding.
And now he was with her.

Chapter 31

I suddenly felt sick to my stomach. Where had they gone?

Troy was punishing me still, and he was doing it with another woman. He was with that woman Susannah, who he was promised to since birth.

Anyone but her, I thought to myself. She was crazy about him, and long had her heart set on marrying him since before she even knew what love was. That was hard to deal with.

When I had gone to the stables to look for him, I assumed he was out there blowing off steam, not galloping around the countryside with another woman. I was raging with jealousy. I had hurt him by letting his brother flirt so aggressively with me and now he was getting back at me. This was part of my punishment, just as last night had been punishment.

This man truly could have any woman he wanted, and he was just toying with me. I would never have him in the true sense, I could never possess him like property, but to be treated this way extremely hard to deal with. My imagination took over and I imagined them riding on horses and laughing through the woods. I imagined that he would lay her down in a spot like we had, and fuck her hard. She would delight in that too. She would feel like she had won. I knew her type, she was desperate for this man, and women in desperation did crazy things. I had to shake those thoughts from my head. I was never good with jealousy; in fact it was a part of my nature I always despised in myself. It caused me so much pain. Even now when trying not to be jealous, thoughts of them together invaded my mind. He was probably fucking her right now.

I couldn't blame him. It had been an emotional few weeks, and I was feeling defeated by it. From the moment we first collided on the street and I spilled coffee on him, it had been a whirlwind. That spilled coffee turned into our wild and unusual sexual escapades, that were emotionally charged and would leave anyone feeling exhausted both physically and mentally.

Now we were on this trip up the Hudson River, in his country cottage. It was a lot to do in such a short amount of time. We had managed to go through so much. It felt like a year of all things emotional squeezed into a few weeks. It was a lot for me and I'm sure it was a lot for him too. I wondered if he'd had enough of me.

Last night's incident with Will felt like the last straw. I was still being punished. What next, I thought? Troy he give me the silent treatment, and if so for how long? Was this the end of our strange and brief affair? Was he making arrangements to send me back to New York?

Not knowing what was going on made me feel anxious and nervous. I didn't know what to do with myself.

I sighed and hated myself for being so stupid to respond to Will's advances, that rogue. Will, that brooding animal who had just as much confidence as Troy, was having the same effect on me.

The though of it was making me want him again. I couldn't figure out why. He reminded me of Troy so much I suppose. It was almost as if they were two variations of the same person. That was a dangerous thought.

I was in this deep now, whatever this was. I had a man punishing me, and acting like a jealous husband. He had introduced me to his family, for some insane reason, but things would be different from now on. I wasn't sure how exactly. He would either want me more or loathe me and leave me. I wasn't prepared for either one. I wished I could take back last night's incident. It had really got to him, and it hurt him. I didn't want to hurt Troy. I had strong feelings for him. But I had to admit, I never thought the fumbling old me who was always late and falling would have such an affect on a handsome and powerfully rich man. A man that had a lot of women at his disposal and who thought I was only using him for sex. It was weird to think of myself from that perspective.

So far nothing had gone the way it was supposed to in a normal relationship. Normal was so far removed from what we were doing, that I didn't even know what that was anymore. It was all so dysfunctional, but that's what our entire relationship had been since day one. If you could call whatever this was a relationship.

I felt exhausted and invigorated by it all at the same time. For now I would go one step at a time. Troy was out of the house doing who knows what with another woman, and I needed to distract myself or I would drive myself crazy with worry. I would take this time for a little me time. I ran a hot bath and soaked in it for an hour. It was a perfect beginning to enjoying a day of me time. If Troy was going to ignore me and do things with another woman then I would turn this place into my own spa.

Chapter 32

After my long bath, I dried my hair and applied all sorts of oils and creams to my face and body. I was giving myself the full treatment. I curled my long hair, polished my toenails.

After, I fixed myself a light breakfast with coffee and ate it upstairs in bed. I didn't want to leave it. The bed felt warm and cozy, and I quickly fell asleep. A few hours later I awoke in the early afternoon. I half expected Troy to be snuggled next to me, but he was not. I freshened up, put on a pretty sweater dress and boots, and went down stairs. Surely he would be back and pouting away in the library. Once again I searched the house. He was nowhere to be found.

So he was going to avoid me. If that's what he needed to do in order for us to get through this then that's what I would endure. I started to think of ways to bide my time in this vast house alone. I went to the vast library. It was a large cavernous room with double rows of books and a ladder that wheeled around all of it. I was overjoyed with it. I really needed to make better use of this? I went over to the windows and opened all of the drapes to let light in. Just then I had a great thought. I would pull a few of these and have a picnic lounging in the grass reading. That was a perfect way to spend the rest of the day. I needed sun and nature.

I went to work getting my perfect picnic together. I browsed around and found a few books for my picnic. I went over to the desk and picked up a few recent magazine editions. I was all set. I grabbed a tote bag and stuffed it with snacks from the fridge and a few books. I grabbed a large blanket and headed out onto the grass. I set up my picnic and laid down. I stared up at the sky and the trees over head. This was a perfect way to spend the day.

I enjoyed it and could see me being the lady of this house. I was content to spend my time here every day for the rest of my life. I froze. Wow, I had never thought that of any place I had ever lived. Everywhere was always sort of an okay for now type of apartment or dwelling. But this, this was a home. A home that generations and generations of Troy's family had lived in. I smiled at the idea of possibly being one of them and relished the thought; maybe I was taking this all this too seriously. The thing really holding me back from really trusting Troy though, was the Amber incident.

I swallowed hard as a light bulb went off in my head. I had actually done worse than that with Will last night. I did exactly what Troy did to me, but so much worse. Amber was my co-worker, not my sister, and it was at a time that we weren't really anything. He had brought me to his home, introduced me to his mother, and that's when the incident with his brother happened.

Putting it into that context made me realize exactly how horrible it was. How horrible I was. I had been more than ready to write him off for hitting on my co-worker, well trying to sleep with her, and yet I expected him to forgive me for doing much the same with his brother?

Yes, it wasn't entirely and identical situation, but close enough. I felt awful. I started to feel angry with myself. Who had I become? This wasn't me. Troy had changed me. I felt like a sex addict. It had become a drug to me, and like any junkie, my behavior had changed for the worse.

I lay back on the blanket and closed my eyes absorbing the sun. The whole day passed and I spent it sunbathing, reading, and eating from the picnic. I watched the birds and squirrels scamper about and butterflies dance in the breeze. It was a true lazy afternoon. I almost didn't want to go inside when the sun began to set. That's when I realized; Troy still had not been back. Would he come back at all tonight?

I stood up to stretch and looked toward the stables to see two riders on one horse galloping toward the stables. It was Troy, and he was with Susannah. She straddled him from behind, holding on to him tightly. What the hell is this? I thought. They didn't even have the decency to take two horses?

He rode the horse into the stable. I wanted to go down there and see what the hell was going on but I didn't. Instead I plopped back down on the blanket and picked up my book. It looked like I was reading but I was peering over the book at the stables.

Fifteen minutes passed and they still had not emerged. Was he fucking her in there? Was this part of my punishment? Had he replaced me already? So many questions swam through my head, and the worst part was not knowing. I needed to know and I needed to know now.

Just then they both emerged from the stable and began to walk toward the house, and toward me. I pretended not to notice. I focused my attention back on my book even though I was just staring at the page and not reading at all.

As they came closer, I looked at my book. I didn't want him to see me looking at them. I flushed, and moved the book higher to hide my face. So that's how he's going to play it. That was fine. I would let him do what he needed to do. I could handle this. I straightened up and squared my shoulders, ready for battle. They finally got closer to the house and looked in my direction. They began to walk toward me. I looked up at them and smiled a fake smile and batted my lashes.

Susannah addressed at me with fake politeness and honeyed tones. "Oh how cute. Look at you. You are so cute in your little dress and your little picnic, just like a child."

Troy laughed. I looked at him, shooting dangers with my eyes but kept a smile on my lips.

He plopped down on the blanket far away from me. "Sit a while Susannah."

She sat very close to Troy, practically on top of him. He grabbed a strawberry and fed it to her. She moaned loudly, tasting it. I wanted to slap it out of his hand. I narrowed my eyes in his direction, but he pretended not to notice. Though I'm sure that he could feel me burning a hole in him. I slammed the book closed.

Troy never looked at me once. I was angry, jealous, and hurt. I reminded myself that he was purposefully punishing me. For what I did with Will. I gathered my courage and said, "Well I was just about to go inside. Try the sandwiches Susannah, they are delicious."

I got up, not making eye contact and walked away. I heard them both laughing as I got further and further away. It stung to hear them enjoying themselves. This was it. He was done with me. I would never be able to have this man. He was unattainable now more than ever. I fought back tears. That's fine. I am better than this. I want him. I need him. But I won't make a fool of myself. I'm not going to beg him. He could do as he pleased, but I was not going to stay around to watch.

Yes, I messed up by allowing his brother to talk to me in that way. But I didn't find someone to flirt with and flaunt it in front of him on purpose. That was cruel.

Chapter 33

I climbed the stairs in silent tears. I just needed to make it to the room and then I could let the floodgates open.

I made it inside the room and threw myself on the bed and cried. I realized, I was hurt, because I loved him. That was a sobering and disturbing thought.

There was no other explanation though. A bruised ego wouldn't hurt this much, therefore it must be love. How stupid was I to fall in love with a powerful millionaire that would forever be a bachelor? Yes, we shared a passionate lust, but that did not mean that he loved me, cared about me even.

There was a knock at the door. I didn't answer and Troy didn't bother to open the door. He just yelled through it, "Olivia, we're eating dinner in thirty minutes." Then he walked away.

The anger welled up inside of me. I thought I could take this but I couldn't. Clearly, Troy wasn't going to stop with this. I don't know how long this would go on. Would he expect me to endure months of him treating me badly? I thought it would pass, but now he wanted me to join him and that woman for dinner. I wouldn't do it. In fact, I could just leave. That thought made me sit up immediately. I could leave. There was nothing holding me here. I could go and be somewhere free of this treatment. I would lose Troy, but I felt like I already had, the way he was behaving. Did I really have him anyway? I never had his heart.

That was it, my mind was made up, and I was leaving. I grabbed the phone and called for a cab. I locked the door, and went to the closet. Most of this stuff was not mine anyway, all gifts from Troy. So it would be easy to pack. I would get back to living in anonymity and just be me in New York. Susannah could now congratulate herself as she had won, and Troy was all hers. That little stunt earlier with the strawberry had the outcome they wanted. They won.

I packed fast. I put on my coat and was ready to head downstairs. I looked around the room and took in one last deep breath. I wanted to burn the memory of this place into my mind. Then I sighed and headed to the door when there was a loud pounding against it. The knob turned and jiggled.

"Olivia did you call a cab? Olivia open this door."

It was Troy and he was angry. I didn't care. I was still leaving. What did he want to do, force me to spoon-feed his new girl? I wasn't having any of it. I was not playing any games.

"Go away Troy. I'm tired. I'm tired of this. I'm going home."

There was no more pounding at the door, then suddenly there was a loud burst as he kicked the door open. The anger in his eyes scared me. He looked at me and looked at the bag in my hand. I just stared back in shock. His chest heaved aggressively.

"What are you doing? Why did you order a cab?"

"I'm leaving. I let you punish me last night, but now this. Another woman? I won't let you or any man treat me like that. I don't care how much money you have, or how powerful you are. My happiness is more important than money."

"You can't leave. I won't allow it."

"Allow it? Are you listening to yourself? You don't own me. This has gone on far too long. It's a mess. This is not what I want in my life."

There was complete silence. A look of enlightenment came over his face. I didn't know what he was thinking. Did he know I was right? Did he know this was absurd? That we had gone too far in this madness? I continued: "If you really don't want to lose me, than be a damn gentleman. Send that woman away."

"She's already gone." He sat on the edge of the bed.

"What?"

"I did. I did bring her here to make you jealous. I wanted you to see me with her. To know she was a threat. I was going to make you sit and have dinner with us. Then I realized that I cannot stand her. I can't stand that woman, and it was complete torture to be with her today. She pales in comparison to you. We sat down at dinner and when you refused to come down. I sent her away. I'm sorry."

I dropped my bag on the floor.

"Olivia, I'm sorry. I'm sorry. The thing with my brother, it got to me. We don't get along and it's a long-standing feud between us. He's always tried to steal women from me, and has succeeded on occasion, but it's never affected me this way. Until now, and now I'm taking it out on you. I'm so sorry. Please don't leave. I was a jerk. I know. I won't do it again. I can promise you that. Just don't leave."

I looked up at him with tears in my eyes. "I don't want to leave, but you gave me no choice."

"I know I'm sorry." He came over to me on the floor and wrapped his arms around me and rocked me back and forth, consoling me.

Troy grabbed my face in his hands and kissed me. I let go of my anger and sadness and kissed back. He laid me down on the ground, the shattered pieces of door around us.

He put his hands on my dress and pulled it up to my waistline. Troy reached down and opened my thighs. He fingered the fabric of my panties and pushed them to one side. He brought his face down between my legs and licked my slick cleft. I gasped. He licked up and down. I moaned and cried and moaned again. I was filled with emotions and I couldn't control them.

"Olivia. My Olivia. Please stay. Don't leave me. I need you."

I moaned again. I loved hearing him say those words. This was the Troy I loved. This was the man I would stay for, not the angry vengeful man he had shown me.

In no time I was whispering, "I'm coming..."

When I was done having an emotional and heartfelt orgasm, he unzipped his pants and pulled out his hard rod. He massaged it with the palm of his hand. He placed the tip inside me and once again pushed inside me. His manhood filled me. His thick member moved in and out of me fast. The emotions running through us only put me on the brink of another orgasm.

"I love being inside you. You feel so good," Troy whispered in my ear. He grabbed my waist and held me tight as he thrust himself harder and faster inside me. I couldn't handle it anymore and I exploded into an orgasm again. This must have set him off too, because he came almost a few seconds after I did. He stayed inside me for a minute or two, both of us enjoying the remnants of our orgasm.

That night we made love two more times, it was heartfelt and beautiful but we both knew something had changed. This had to end. It was too much for both of us and it was consuming us. The sex and lust that we shared together wasn't enough to sustain a relationship.

The next morning I woke up to an empty house and a note on the pillow.

Chapter 34

Troy was not in my bed and I had hoped that he'd forgiven me for the Will incident, but clearly he had not. Instead he left a note. I looked at the broken door and remembered how exhilarating it was to have him kick it open. I replayed that in my head. A man wouldn't do that unless he had deep feelings for me.

A car will take you back to New York as soon as you're ready.

That's it. That was all that the note said, followed by the number of the car service. I was so confused. I was baffled, and I had to read it a few times to know it was real.

I put on a robe and ran downstairs to see if he was still in the house. He was not. I went outside, the black SUV was gone. This could not be real, I told myself. I sat and stared at the wall trying to process this.

How could he just leave me like this after he begged me not to leave him last night? It didn't make sense. It was insane. Only a crazy person would act this way. The tears came and the floodgates opened. This couldn't be the way things ended, not after all the emotions we went through last night.

I spent nearly an hour crumpled on the foyer of the big house. How had my life become such a mess? Now I was here, abandoned in a vast house in upstate New York. This couldn't be the reality of my life.

At some point, I couldn't cry anymore. There were no tears left. Feeling abandoned had an awful effect on me. My sadness turned to anger and I demanded answers. I called The Plaza hotel operator demanding to be transferred to his private apartment. They refused. I was mortified. I didn't even have his private phone number, just the apartment suite number inside The

Plaza. I only just recently learned his last name was Lane, but that was only because of the family wedding. He never actually told me his last name, or anything for that matter. This was such a backwards way of falling for someone. It was the most painful and yet pleasurable exquisite mix of love and the erotic.

It was too much.

The wedding ... His brother — was this more punishment? Was last night only a pretend apology to get me to stay here because he wanted to be the one to leave? I wouldn't put it past Troy to think in those terms.

That must be it. This is more punishment. I was sure he would be back later tonight. I just knew it. He was a jerk for doing this to me, but clearly the incident with his brother was a major trigger for him. I wondered if the whole family knew? All his relations probably thought me of as a whore now, but that thought didn't bother me. Troy had tried to punish me with his former girlfriend, or betrothed or what ever she was, but he couldn't because he didn't enjoy her company. So now he was using abandonment as a punishment. I now saw it all so clearly.

I wouldn't let him know he'd won though.

The front door rang. I secretly hoped it was Troy returning and I answered only to find it was an old handy man. He had come to fix the broken bedroom door.

Seems that Troy had taken care of everything as if I wasn't even here.

I let the guy in and offered to lead him to the door. He knew exactly what to do; he had worked on the house for years.

A few hours later he left and a brand new door was installed with a new lock. I was sad to see the evidence of Troy's passionate reaction gone. I liked seeing the door that way.

No one had ever broken down doors for me before.

After the guy left, I grabbed a bottle of brandy and began to drink. An hour later I was a mess.

I went into the library and started digging through drawers. I didn't know what I was looking for specifically, but basically any way I could contact Troy.

Surely, there would be a cell phone bill in here or something of that sort? It even crossed my mind to contact his mother, or question the foreman in the stables for information.

Those thoughts however made me feel like a crazy woman, and I was already losing myself by snooping through the library. I opened a drawer on the large heavy oak desk. It was full of stuff and disorganized. I fumbled through it and finally lost my nerve. I pulled the drawer completely out of the desk and empty the contents of it on the floor.

I collapsed to the ground in a heap of exhaustion and drunkenness. Then the doorbell rang again and I popped up in surprise. Who could that be this time? Was it the car service? Had he ordered them to force me to leave the house?

Or was it Troy with an apology and flowers. But no it couldn't be. It was his house; obviously he would use his key. At that last thought I heard the door open and close. I began to panic. Who could it be? I was sure I locked the door. I heard a deep voice echo in the large hall.

"Troy?"

I recognized the voice immediately. It was the same voice that had whispered tantalizing words in my ear only days before.

Chapter 35

"Well, isn't this a sight," Will said as he looked at me on the ground on top of a mess of papers and items I had dumped from the desk.

I was still in a robe and had not brushed my hair or cleaned the mascara tears off my face. I looked a complete mess.

I narrowed my eyes, hating him. He was the reason for this. He laughed and said, "Where's my brother? I've come to apologize."

"He went back to the city. He left me." I said, in barely a whisper.

"I see ..." He leaned against the doorway and arrogantly crossed his arms. I tried to ignore how magnetic he was. "Why is that?" he asked.

I looked at him and my annoyance and drunkenness took over me. I stood up and went over to him, "You know why. This is your fault." I slapped him across the face.

His face turned at the force of the slap, but then he simply turned back toward me and grinned. It didn't even phase him. "Why? Why did he leave?" he asked again.

"Because of you," I barked. "Because of what happened. The things you did to me. The things you said."

He lowered his gaze, all innocence. "What did I say?"

A flood of all the things he had actually said suddenly came back to me. It was like I was back in that moment all over again. Him whispering in my ear about his hard cock, and putting it in my mouth, and I now felt aroused again.

"Say it. Say I asked if you wanted me to put my cock in your mouth," he said slowly and seductively.

My breathing increased. I was in a fragile and lonely state of abandonment, and his words were like a junkie getting their fix. It was too much. I lifted my hand to strike him again, but he caught it before it hit his face. He grabbed my hand and turned it over and kissed the inside of my palm. I moaned instinctively. His eyes brightened at my reaction.

"You want me Olivia. You want me to fuck you. You want my hard cock, and you want me to do things to you. I can feel you now. You're wet aren't you? I don't need to touch you to know that you're wet."

I closed my eyes and let a tear escape down my cheek. He was right, and I hated him for being right. I had become an addict to this type of pleasure. Once I got a taste of being talked to like this I couldn't stop it.

I couldn't stop myself. I opened my eyes and looked up at him. He leaned over and kissed me on the lips. They were soft and full and the kiss was slow and sensual.

Will wrapped his arms around me and rubbed my back, sliding his hands down to my buttocks. He squeezed them and let out a moan. Then he pulled away from me and looked down at me with his green eyes. They were piercing through me and my mouth watered as I looked at his perfect face.

His square jaw was masculine and the just right amount of stubble shaded it. His thick hair was unkempt and shaggy and he looked like a more wild and outdoorsy version of Troy. Like a lumberjack that only cared about the primitive necessities in life.

Sex being one of them.

He ran his thumb across my bottom lip and said, "I can't wait to slide my thick hard cock inside your mouth. Do you want to suck on it? Hmm...Do you? I know you do."

My breath caught in my throat. I was excited, even through my drunken haze, this was affecting me. I didn't even make a decision, my body made it for me. I put my hands on his chest and felt his hard taught body underneath his plaid blue and white shirt. He looked rugged, like a man, a real man.

It was hard to not touch him. He grabbed my hands and took them off his chest. I was confused and felt rejected, but then he grabbed the belt of my robe and pulled it, untying it slowly. I swallowed hard. He lifted one side of the robe and opened it and looked at my naked body.

Then he ran his hand through my long hair, and then he grabbed it and pulled at it. My head titled back, and my eyes opened wide. I felt a little scared to be alone with this stranger and he was going to do as he pleased with me. That thought made me feel excited though. I opened my mouth and he crushed his lips on top of mine. He explored my mouth, keeping one hand in my hair and the other on my waist. Then he pulled away and said, "I'm going to show you what it's like to be with a real man."

Chapter 36

He grabbed the robe and aggressively ripped it off me. My breasts heaved up and down with my ragged breath. My nipples were hard and aroused.

Will put his hands on my bottom and picked me up. I wrapped my legs around him and he carried me to the cluttered desk. I felt like a whore. I was about to let this man, who was the brother of man I thought I loved fuck me. And I wanted it badly. The realization dawned on me, I felt like a whore, because I *was* a whore. This is what a whore did.

"What do you think I'm going to do to you?" he asked.

"I don't know," I whispered.

"Yes, you do. Say it," he commanded.

"You're going to fuck me," I breathed.

"I might," he said. "If I think you deserve it." He put his hands on my knees and parted my legs. He took one finger and ran it upwards. I moaned in response. Then he said, "Open your mouth."

I did as he said and he put the same finger in my mouth. I could taste myself.

"Good girl," he said. "Now put your hands on the desk and lean back."

I did as he said. I put my hands on top of the mess I had created. I placed my palms down on the desk behind me and leaned back.

"Good," Will said. Then he grabbed one leg and bent it at the knee and placed my foot on the edge of the desk. Then he grabbed the other and did the same thing. I felt so vulnerable in this position. I was completely naked and he was still clothed. I felt like a sex doll that he was putting into a position of his liking.

Perhaps the worse thing about it was that I loved this. I truly loved every second of it. The anticipation was like fuel to a fire burning in me. He took a few steps back and looked at me like he was admiring a painting he was working on. It was unsettling and exciting. I grew wetter and wetter by the second.

Being on display like this reminded me of the first time Troy and I were together and I stood over the bed. That thought hit me like a ton of bricks. I felt a sobering calm come over me. I looked at Will. I put my legs down and sat up. The look of desire on his face changed to pure confusion. Without a word I got up from the desk and walked over to my robe on the ground. I put it back on and tied it tightly around my waist.

I looked back at Will. His mouth was open and his hands were out with his palms up, as if to say what the hell? I tried my utmost to ignore the aching bulge in his jeans and how it was making me feel. God, I wanted that inside me. Wanted him to fuck me hard.

But somehow I found the words. "It's your brother I want, not you. Please leave."

Then I turned and hurried upstairs, my legs throbbing with lust and fear. Fear that I wouldn't have the strength to keep going. Fear that I would lose it, run straight back there and impale myself on what I knew would be his magnificent cock.

I locked the door to the bedroom just in case. I didn't trust myself or him.

But then seconds later, I recognized the reality of the situation. Troy had left me, abandoned me here in this house, miles away from home.

Clearly he didn't care what I did or what I wanted.

Whereas downstairs there was a man, a smoldering brute who was very clear about what he wanted to do to me. I was already paying the price for my previous encounter with Will so did it matter if this time we truly got to finish things off properly?

Finish one another off properly...

My lips were wet as I thought about going back down there and just jumping on Will's glorious cock. I ached to feel its throbbing thickness inside me, was desperate for him to fuck me until I no longer knew my own name.

We had the house all to ourselves; we could pleasure each other for hours on the desk, the stairs, the kitchen countertop, wherever the hell we liked.

And I knew we would be incredible together, downstairs just now had been a mere teaser.

At this point I could almost feel his cock buried inside me and knew I couldn't stand to keep away from him any longer.

I knew that the sex would be earth-shattering - incredible - and oh God I was already close to orgasm at the very idea of taking him in my mouth and sucking...

My legs felt like jelly as I moved to the door. I knew that the decision I made next would change things forever.

A vision in my head of me sprawled face down across the kitchen countertop, Will ramming into me from behind, sent a trickle of moisture down the side of my leg, and a fresh wave of longing burned through me.

I reached for the door handle.

It was time to choose between my heart or my desire.

Part 3

Chapter 37

My hand reached for the key in my bedroom door, as I tried to decide.

I loved Troy, but right then I wanted his brother Will so badly I could almost taste him. I didn't think my body would let me resist him.

But right then, I heard the screeching of tires from outside.

I exhaled, realizing the decision had already been made for me. Will had left.

I pulled myself together and took a long hot shower. This was crazy. I was finished here. I would go back to the city. I needed comfort and I needed my friend.

Then an idea hit me.

I quickly got out of the shower and grabbed the note that Troy had left for me about the car taking me wherever I wanted to go whenever. I called the company and learned that Troy had told them to bill all that I needed to his account. Perfect, I thought as I hung up. I would let them know I would be calling back with an address in ten minutes for a pick up.

I dialed Lily in New York, and invited her to come out for a visit. She was thrilled to get away from the bustling busy chaos and to come visit me in the countryside for the weekend. I didn't tell her the truth of course, I simply told her Troy went out of town and encouraged me to make myself at home.

Which he had, in a way.

I called the car service and put in a request to pick up Lily in the city the next day and bring her to the house. Then I called the local market and had an enormous amount of groceries delivered. The house also had a running tab with the market as well.

I was feeling better already.

Chapter 38

The next morning I awoke bright an early and stretched out in the bed. I rolled over expecting to feel Troy next to me. Then I remembered, he had left, and I once again felt bereft.

No, you're not doing this again. I told myself. You mourned yesterday and now it's time to get back to your life.

I forced myself out of bed and freshened up. I put on a pair of skinny jeans, a warm comfy sweater and thick plush socks and boots.

Lily would be arriving in a little under two hours, if traffic was good, and I wanted her to feel like she was on vacation. I wanted to feel that way as well. I needed this as much, if not more than, she did. I wanted to forget about everything that happened and use this weekend to reset myself. I would forget that this was Troy's house and would pretend it was simply a vacation rental.

I went downstairs and made coffee. I poured myself a large mug and went into the library. It was still a huge mess. Will's face and my naked body sprawled beneath him on the desk flashed before me.

What a crazy life I was living, I thought to myself as I shoved everything back into the drawers and made the library presentable again.

I didn't care if things weren't in order. At this point I really had no cares at all. I had no fear. It was though I had hit rock bottom last night and the only way I could go now, was up.

I went outside and made little bouquets of orange and gold leaves and white wild flowers from the grounds and placed them in vases around the house. Including my room, the guest room for Lily, and the dining table. This felt good. I felt in control again.

The groceries arrived and I set about putting things away. I started on a delicious hearty lunch for the two of us. I turned on the sound system and blasted some cheesy hits from the 1980s. I put a small chicken in the oven with sweet potatoes and carrots.

An hour later, Lily arrived.

I gave her the grand tour of the house and she looked at everything with wide eyes.

"Olivia, this place is absolutely incredible! And it's enormous, no wonder you sent for me, I wouldn't want to be here alone either."

I faked a smile through that last comment, if she only knew the extent of, and reason for my loneliness.

"This is your room," I said as I led her to a gorgeous room with a canopy bed draped in white lace. It had its own Juliette style balcony with French glass doors to the outside, and offered a view of a small pond in the distance.

"Make yourself at home. I'm going to go check on lunch. I'll be in the kitchen when you're ready."

"Okay, I'll unpack and freshen up and then I'll be down."

I left Lily to enjoy her new room and went to the kitchen. I opened the oven and inhaled the aroma of our lunch. It was done. I grabbed a few oven mitts and pulled the dish out, and then the phone rang. It was the landline ringing in the kitchen. Strange I thought, though I guessed I should answer it.

"Hello?" I said into the handset.

There was silence on the other end of the line. I said hello again but still no answer, then whoever it was hung up the line. I hung up the phone. Either it was Troy calling to see if I was still at the house, or it was Will, who realized I was still here.

I thought of the dangerous game I was playing, just by being at this house. The brothers came from a powerful and rich family; surely they were not people to mess around with as I currently was. Those dark thoughts were swimming through my mind when I heard, "It smells amazing."

Lily was standing in the doorway. "I'm famished. The traffic getting out of Manhattan was hell. I thought I would never get here."

"Well I'm glad you are here. I've missed you. Now, let's eat."

We sat down at the kitchen table and made light conversation. Lily filled me in on her latest headlines in her life; the basics of work, dating, and her apartment. These were the normal things good friends would discuss and my heart yearned for those basic things. I missed my normal life before Troy entered it. I longed for my most serious concern to be only that of worrying about being late to work.

Now my life was so complicated and ... full of crazy drama.

I listened to every detail of Lily's chat. I needed to visualize her easygoing life and get lost in it.

Before I knew it we were stuffed with our heavy lunch.

"I feel like I'm going to explode," she said.

"Well, I have just the thing for that."

"What?"

"We can go for a stroll in the woods. This property is absolutely stunning, you have to see it," I said.

"Well, all right - as long as you promise me it is a stroll and not a hike. Just a light ramble to digest."

I laughed at her and said, "I promise."

I put the leftovers in the fridge and we grabbed our coats and scarves and headed out into the bright sunlight of the day. It was a beautiful cloudless afternoon. We strolled the property and visited the stables, feeding the horses hay from our hands and giggling like a couple of school girls. It was fun. It was innocent and it was just what I needed.

Chapter 39

That night we decided to take a cab into the small town nearby.

We walked around, window shopping and enjoying the night air. Tarrytown was very cute and quaint. It was old and had that New England charm to it. We walked down Main Street and soon worked up an appetite. We happened upon a local spot called Horsefeathers, an adorable warm and cosy pub. We ate greasy bar food and drank many pints of beer.

We got lost in girl talk until the bartender came over to us with two more drinks.

"We didn't order these," I pointed out.

"They're from the gentleman over there," he said pointing to the corner of the pub. Lily and followed his gaze and saw a man sitting in the corner.

My heart almost stopped.

"Oh, he's hot," Lily gasped, grinning.

I swallowed hard. "That's Troy's brother."

"Oh, then you have to introduce me," she said.

"I don't know him that well ..." I mumbled, trying to figure out a way we could avoid Will completely. I couldn't let Lily find out what had happened a couple of nights ago at the house. I certainly didn't trust him to keep a secret.

And even worse, I still didn't know how to feel about it all.

But it was too late. He was already on his way over.

"Hey, Olivia. How are you? You look amazing," he said with a cocky grin.

I stared up at him in silence. My tongue could not seem to work.

On the other hand, Lily dove right in, "Hello there, I'm Lily."

Will grabbed her hand and kissed it lightly. "Will Lane, very nice to meet you."

He gave her that look. That seductive look that said he wanted to fuck her.

Instantly I felt jealous, but tried to bat the feeling away. What was the hell was wrong with me? Despite what had gone wrong between us, it was Troy I wanted, Troy I loved.

"I'm staying with Olivia over the weekend," Lily was saying. "You should come visit," she added coquettishly.

She was bold, I thought. Though she was on vacation and girls on vacation had nothing to lose and were short on time.

"How about now?" he suggested. He sat down close beside her and I watched as he easily seduced her with his sensual looks and words.

I knew exactly what this was leading to and I was powerless to stop it. I caught him looking at me a few times with that cocky smirk on his face. I wanted to slap him again, slap that grin off his face and force him to leave, but that would be revealing too much. I'm sure he knew this and kept playing this game. It was exciting to him. We finished our drinks and Lily kept encouraging him to join us at the house.

Chapter 40

Fifteen minutes later we were all squeezed into a cab. Back at the house, I went straight into the kitchen and drank a large amount of water. I knew better than to be drunk around Will. It was something I had learned from my past mistakes. I concentrated hard on sobering up. I could hear him and Lily laughing in the hallway. They both came into the kitchen.

"I am very tired. I'm going to go to bed," I said. I gave Lily a kiss on the cheek.

"Are you sure? It's still so early," she said, though her eyes shone with excitement and desire as she stood alongside Will.

I recognized that look all too well.

"I woke up very early this morning so I'm done. But please you two enjoy yourselves," I added with a pasted-on smile. I excused myself and went to my room.

I got ready for bed and slipped under the covers.

A few minutes later, from somewhere else in the house, I heard Lily yelling out in ecstasy. I heard something like a piece of furniture, perhaps a headboard hitting the wall, and then I heard him groaning too. Another surge of jealousy welled up in me, as I tried to imagine what it must be like to be fucked by Will, as I almost had the other night.

Then I once again reminded myself that I wanted Troy. Even though he'd abandoned me, I still hoped things would be different eventually.

I couldn't listen to this all night though. It made me feel lonely as well as a host of other emotions I didn't want. I grabbed a pair of headphones and fell asleep to music.

This wasn't exactly turning out to be the ideal girl's weekend, but it was what it was.

The next morning I awoke bright and early. I remembered Will was in the house. I didn't want to leave my room so I stayed in bed as long as I could. Then there was a knock at the door.

"Yes?"

"It's Lily, come down for breakfast."

"Okay, I'll be right there."

I was relieved to hear she was awake so I didn't run the risk of facing Will alone while she slept. I put on some clothes and went down to the kitchen. I was delighted to find that she seemed to be on her own.

"Where's Will?" I asked.

"I walked him out about an hour ago," she said with a huge smile on her face. "He went to the stables before he left to talk to the foreman."

"Oh?" I said, trying to hold back my fear. I really didn't want anyone from the staff to know that Will had been here while I was here. It made me feel uneasy.

"Olivia?" Lily pulled me out of my concentrated thoughts.

"Yes?" I said.

"I had the best sex of my life," she said laughing. "I never thought it could be like that. He is handsome and so sexual. It was wild and ... primitive, almost. God, it was amazing."

"That's great," I said faking enthusiasm, though in truth I was happy for me friend. Why shouldn't she have some excitement?

Though she went on to tell me every little detail of their encounter. None of it surprised me, given my own experiences with Will. She told me about how he dominant he was, commanding her to do things that thrilled her. She told me about how he knew a woman's body like no other man she had ever been with.

Listening to her made me miss Troy more than ever.

And wonder what I had missed by denying Will.

Chapter 41

A few hours later, Lily and I went riding. The foreman, Mr. Grace was nice enough to escort us. It was a nice relaxing day. I enjoyed nature and my friend's company and I was happy to know that according to Lily, Will would not be coming back that evening.

Instead we had a true girl's night. We binged on ice cream and cake and made homemade facial masks. We watched movies in front of the fireplace and fell asleep under a pile of blankets and pillows.

The next morning we packed up to leave. I took one last brief stroll around the property. I was sad to leave the place. Since Troy never came back like I thought he would, it really felt like it was over. My heart felt heavy with that thought.

I was nervous the entire ride back to New York. I had only been gone a couple of weeks, but it felt like a lifetime.

I didn't know if I knew how to just be me again.

I walked into my apartment and felt a wave of relief come over me. I threw myself on my bed and enjoyed the comfort of it. This was mine and this is where I lived my life. A life that I absolutely needed to get back to if I was going to stay sane.

With that I picked up the phone and called work. My transfer had finally gone through and I would be working at a different branch of the spa.

I was excited, and I was needed the very next day. That was perfect I thought, I needed to be busy as soon as possible.

I unpacked my bags and cleaned the dust off of everything. I watched a few episodes of bad television and went to bed early.

Tomorrow was the start of a new phase in my life and I wanted to be well rested for it.

The next morning I awoke to a loud buzz. I grabbed my alarm and turned it off. In my sleepy state it took me a minute to realize that it wasn't my alarm, but my door buzzer. I looked at the time, it was four o' clock in the morning.

What the hell was going on? It must be someone that had the wrong apartment, or maybe a thief trying to make his way in? I went to the intercom "Hello?"

"Let me in." I heard the voice say. My heart dropped to my stomach.

Troy. I paused and let all these emotions run through me. I wanted him. I missed him.

But he turned my life upside down and I was trying to get it back on track.

"Go away. Leave me alone." I said, loud and clear. I was shaking and trembling as I backed away from the intercom. I didn't let him talk anymore. I went back to my bed. He rang the buzzer for ten more minutes before it was silent again. I poured myself a glass of red wine to calm my nerves and help myself go back to sleep. In the morning I awoke and remembered what had happened. I questioned whether it had really happened or if I had dreamt it.

What could he possibly want with me now? Did he find about what I let his brother do to me at the house? Was he here to get angry with me and to punish me more? Did he want me back in his life?

I shook all these thoughts from my mind. He was doing it; he was already affecting me, and distracting me. I wouldn't let it happen. I jumped out of bed and got ready for my first day of work at the new branch. I was not going to revert back to my old ways and be late. I rushed around and gave myself plenty time to get to work. I went outside and hailed a cab. I was on my way and feeling good.

Chapter 42

I arrived fifteen minutes early for work and secretly congratulated myself for being so early. I walked in and was introduced to the staff. It was a very busy day and it was wonderful to have operations and schedules feel my thoughts. I wanted basics and plain work. It was good. Around lunch, that all came crashing down.

"Olivia, there's a delivery for you." The front desk girl told me as me passed me in the hall.

"Okay thanks I'll be right up," I went to the front desk expecting an envelope or other work related package being delivered by a courier. Instead there was a large bouquet of yellow and orange roses. My heart pumped fast. I didn't need to look at the card to know whom they were from. I faked a smile and delight in receiving them.

"Thank you. They are beautiful," I told the delivery guy and carried them to my office. I might as well get it over with. I closed the door and opened the card. It read, "Talk to me. You owe me that much."

I shook my head at Troy's words. I owed him nothing, and had no idea what he meant by any of it.

Unless he'd found out about Will's visit.

It didn't matter though; I wasn't getting involved in this again. I crumpled the card and threw it in the trash. Then I remembered I was in a mostly female workplace. I dug it out of the trash and put it in my purse. I didn't need anyone snooping in my business. I was the new girl and everyone was curious about me. I didn't need to give them anything to gossip about.

By the end of the day the words on the card had driven me nearly insane. I heard them over and over again in my head. I stayed late, simply because I didn't want to go home. I organized my office and created the schedule for the entire week. I left fairly late and grabbed the flowers on my way out.

Once I got to my apartment I trashed them. I was content to forget about Troy and clear my mind. My subconscious however kept making him appear in my dreams.

I ignored it.

Chapter 43

Three weeks later I was back in a normal routine. I was rushing around all over Manhattan with a purpose. I went to yoga classes weekly.

I threw myself into my new job, and I went out with Lily every weekend.

It was Friday night and we planned to go to Brooklyn to check out a new hip and trendy bar.

We got on the L train and made our way to Williamsburg. It was a refreshing change to be around the young and cool artists. I was ordering a drink at the bar when a guy approached me, "Can I buy you a drink?" he asked.

I studied my suitor. He was tall and lean with long hair and blue eyes. He had a full beard and wore a t-shirt and a hoodie. He was cute and adorable in a boyish sort of way.

"Sure," I said. "I'll have a martini. Dirty."

He grinned at me and ordered my drink.

"I've never seen you at this bar before."

"I don't normally come to Brooklyn. I live in Manhattan."

"Nice," he said.

We made small talk at the bar. I looked over at Lily who was on the dance floor with a guy. She seemed occupied so I continued my flirtation. His name was Harley, and he was a website designer. A few drinks later I was walking up the stairs of his apartment in Bushwick.

This was good for me I thought. My first distraction, and the first man I would be with since Troy. I walked into his bedroom and stripped. Harley took a step back. "Wow," he said.

Harley stumbled around and made his way to the bed. He was clearly taken aback and watching him react to my sexual confidence was cute to watch, but it wasn't making me aroused. He clumsily took off all his clothes. Then he grabbed a condom and came over to the bed. Climbing on top he put his hard cock inside me then buried his face in my neck and moved in and out.

I lay there, completely unmoved.

"How does that feel?" I asked, trying to insert some excitement into the encounter. He didn't answer me though and just continued to move in and out. I willed myself to try to enjoy it.

Harley was cute and very different, but this was a disaster. I didn't feel in the least bit aroused. It felt so basic and ordinary, a run of the mill one-night stand, and I realized that sexually I was way beyond that.

A few minutes later Harley orgasmed, rolled off me, then quickly fell asleep. I quietly got dressed and snuck out of his apartment. I grabbed a cab and went home. I took a long shower and felt an overwhelming sadness.

I wanted Troy back, and nothing else would ever satisfy me. He had trained me to be his erotic sex toy. It was like he had created a monster. I now had a hunger than only he could satisfy.

I felt very alone in this for the first time. The distractions that I had created lately were not working for me. I spent so much time building a routine and a new life for myself. I had been working hard and filling my days with normal activities, but it wasn't enough. I was fooling myself.

I needed more.

The next day I slept in late. I wanted to spend my Saturday watching movies, ordering pizza, and feeling sorry for myself. It felt good to be in my little cave and hiding from the world. I spent the weekend like this and went back to work on Monday.

I wasn't expecting an eventful day, but it was.

In the lobby, I was arranging the merchandise and some new products when I heard a voice from behind.

"Hello Olivia."

The hair on the back of my neck stood up. I didn't bother to turn around. I knew who it was.

"Look at me," he said.

I turned around and Troy stood there in a dark Armani suit. My stomach filled with butterflies and my heart picked up at speed. He was stunning.

He was gorgeous. He flashed that delicious blinding grin, and I almost had to fight back tears at what he was already doing to my body without laying a finger on me.

"What are you doing here? Do you have an appointment?"

"No, I came to see you."

"Can I help you?" The receptionist asked then, entering the room.

"Yes, I would like a massage, if you have any openings?"

My eyes grew wide. I couldn't stand the thought of him naked, with another woman's hands all over him. It reminded me of the incident with Amber.

"I think we are full just now, but let me check," she said.

"I can help him. He's a friend of mine. Follow me," I said in one quick response. I didn't make eye contact with her, as I didn't want her to read me.

I took him into a massage room and whispered, "What are you doing?"

"Just like old times," Troy said, grinning.

I narrowed my eyes. I wanted to be mad at him, but I couldn't.

"Get undressed and lay the towel over you. I'll be back in a few minutes," I said trying to go through the motions of a professional.

A few minutes later I walked back into the room, he was laying belly down on the table with the towel covering him. I wanted him. I was instantly aroused as soon as he walked into reception earlier. I wanted him to touch me.

It was going to be hard to concentrate, and hard not to chew him out for leaving me at the house with only a note on the pillow.

But I couldn't go there because I knew I would falter, and that was unacceptable at work.

I poured warm oil in my hands and began to massage him. I worked on his back and rubbed down his entire body. He moaned under my touch and it was hard not to kiss every inch of him.

"That feels so good," he said. "Can I turn over?" He grinned up at me and turned sideways. I looked down and saw his glorious cock peeking out. He was naked and very, very hard. My mouth instinctively dropped open as my body instinctively craved to feel it inside me.

"You're hard." I said in a whisper. And I was wet. Very wet.

"I'm hard for you."

I sighed. He was so hot and I longed for him. I wanted him so so badly. I rubbed oil into his chest and belly. Then, unable to help myself any longer, I put both of my hands on his cock and squeezed it. He moaned.

"Shhh..." I said and gently massaged it. I liked having him in my hands. I wanted to make him come. I rubbed up and down slowly, massaging the tip in slow sensual circles. I loved looking at his body. I missed this so much. He moaned with pleasure and I saw that he was resisting the urge to yell out. I stopped massaging him and looked at the clock.

"Hour's up." I gave him a robe and left the room.

I smiled at myself. I got satisfaction out of leaving Troy wanting more. I liked not satisfying him. It felt empowering.

And I instinctively knew that it wasn't over.

Chapter 44

Later that night, he proved me right. My buzzer rang. I didn't bother to answer I just let him in.

Troy walked in. We didn't speak a single word. He grabbed me and kissed me, then picked me up like a baby and threw me on the bed.

I gasped and he kissed me harder. Then he stripped me of my clothes and ran his hands all over my body. I melted into the sheets. He pushed two fingers inside me, then turned me over and laid me on my stomach, entering me from behind. I let him push himself deeper and deeper inside me.

He slammed against me and I enjoyed hearing the smacking contact of our skin colliding. I was deeply entranced in lust and passion.

I was on the brink of orgasm. I felt Troy lean his face on my back and trail kisses on my skin. My whole body shuddered as I let go into orgasm.

Feelings of ecstasy flowed through me and I desperately wanted to shout, "I love you," but I kept it inside. Troy moved fast and faster, sliding in and out of me. Then he finally exploded. After a minute or two, he pulled out of me and sat on the edge of the bed. I looked at him, and my eyes watered over. I couldn't believe this man was back in my life. I glowed with post-coital happiness.

We sat in silence. I wanted to say so much, but I couldn't speak. I was too full of emotion. Then, I didn't get a chance to. Troy got dressed and left. Neither of us had spoken a single word.

Chapter 45

Troy visited my place of work two more times over the next week. He requested me as his masseuse but I came up with an excuse every time.

I was hurt after he left me. I had wanted to talk things through, and he just left me in my apartment that night. It felt so cold.

Now I couldn't think about anything else except being with him again. I thought about him constantly, including our time on his yacht when we had so much fun. I was once again infatuated. The way he made me feel was what I craved on a daily basis. I wanted more and more of it. This was the type of passion I wanted to share with someone. It was what I wanted and needed but I couldn't let him know that. It felt like a game, and my capitulation would be letting him win.

I had to decide if letting him win was more important than denying myself his presence.

I finally couldn't handle it. I found myself walking around Central Park and slowly making my way to The Plaza Hotel. I stood outside across the street staring at the beautiful hotel. This was where it all started. I closed my eyes and could see him sitting across from me in the Palm Court of the hotel lobby. It all played out in my head. It was too much. I walked in the hotel and went up to his apartment. I knocked on the door. There was no answer. I knocked again. I finally gave up and started walking down the hallway. Then I heard the door open behind me.

"Olivia?"

I turned to see Troy staring at me. He was wet with a towel wrapped around his waist. He had obviously been in the shower. I went back to him and stood in the doorway.

"Can I come in?"

He led me inside. "Please sit down, can I get you anything?"

"I guess a drink would be nice."

He poured me a glass of whiskey on ice.

"Thank you," I said as I drank it.

We were silence for a minute and his half naked body in front of me was incredible distracting. He was wet and I wanted to touch him. I diverted my eyes, took a deep breath and began to say what I came to say.

"I miss you, Troy. I don't know what you are doing or what you are thinking, but I can't do this anymore. I've fallen for you. You are all I think about. I was so hurt when you left me at the house in Tarrytown. It was so confusing and I don't know why you did it. Now it doesn't matter. I need you."

I looked up at him with tears in my eyes. He sat down next to me and took the glass out of my hand and placed it on the table.

"Olivia, this has been the hardest few weeks of my life. I thought it was too complicated to be with you. I had never had so much emotional strife in my life. That day I woke up and saw the bedroom door busted open ...it was a sobering thing to look at. I had never acted so angry in my life. You bring that out in me, and I ran away from that. But now I've realized I can't be without you either. I've tried. I've tried and tried again."

I threw myself in his arms and hugged him tightly. The words he said were like angels singing in my ears. It was everything I wanted to hear. I loved it and I loved him, but I had heard this before. The night before he left me in the house he said these same things, yet he left me without a word the next day.

Just disappeared, and I couldn't trust him now because of it. I guess that was just something that I would have to live with if I wanted to be with him. I forced myself to be in the moment.

He covered his mouth with mine and kissed me softly and slowly. "Olivia, I need you Olivia. My heart longs for you."

We embraced each other and cuddled on the bed. We talked for a while about dreams, the future, and traveling to exotic places. Then we began to talk about how life is short and this brought us both to the brink of desire. Reminding ourselves that we are here now, and that the "now" moments are what matter most. This really got us both excited. Troy rolled over onto his side and looked at me, then he said my name again as he caressed my body, "Olivia." He loved saying it and I loved hearing it. He leaned down and kissed me.

Soon our bodies were intertwined. He rolled on top of me and began to rub against me. I could feel that he was hard through my clothes. We were breathing heavily. He kissed my neck and raised his hand to my breast. He fondled it, gently squeezing it in his hand, massaging and kneading. Troy pulled down the delicate material of my silk dress and exposed my hard nipple. He moaned as he looked at the rose colored tip. He ran his thumb across my taught nipple a few times, thoroughly enjoying looking at it. A soft moan left my lips, barely a whisper of a moan. Then he lowered his head onto my chest and wrapped his mouth around my entire breast. His tongued flicked at my nipple.

I looked down at him and wrapped my fingers around his hair. He opened his eyes and looked up at me as he worked with his mouth. He was making me feel so wet I thought I could climax with just this small amount of foreplay. It was Troy that made me feel this way. No other man had ever had this effect on me. It was his energy mixed with the intense anticipation I had felt waiting for this moment. It was our energies combining.

This was meant to be.

Troy pulled himself up and stared at me. He placed his hand on my belly and slowly rubbed down the length of it to my thigh. He pulled up my slip exposing my naked bottom half to the night. He looked down at the wetness between my legs and put his fingers inside me. A look of surprise briefly came across his face, and then he moaned and said,

"You're so wet."

"It's you, you do this to me," I said in a soft barely audible tone.

He bit his lower lip at my reply and then watched his hand as he moved his fingers in and out of me. He liked to watch his work. And I was more than okay with this. It made me feel beautiful. It made me feel desirable. I arched my back in rhythm with his hands and closed my eyes and let him fully enjoy watching me. Finally he stopped and climbed on top of me. He grabbed a condom and pulled it over his perfectly sculpted thick, long, shaft. I wanted to put my mouth around it, but there was no time for that. I needed him inside me at that very moment. I couldn't wait any longer. I had been waiting so long for this and I couldn't put it off any longer.

"I want you inside me," I said.

"You do?" He said, and then added, "How bad do you want it?"

Oh God, he was teasing me. I couldn't handle it. I wanted to beg him for it. I just looked at him and bit my lip to prevent myself from begging. He lowered himself between my legs and inserted just the tip of his cock. I moaned. It felt so good even just this little taste. It was completely clear though, he had the upper hand, and I was at his mercy. I wanted him, needed him, and I had to have him. He played with this idea, looking at me, knowing that I wanted it. He moved just the tip in and out of me. Forever teasing me, it was all I could do not to scream in pleasure.

Then I had enough, I was taking control, and in one quick move I wrapped my legs around him and pushed him in. This caught him completely off guard. I sheepishly smiled and congratulated myself. He was stone frozen. He shifted a little and had to stop. I thought that maybe I had injured him, but as he began to move I heard why he was frozen.

He moaned and looked at me and said, "You're so tight. I missed you so much."

He moaned again as if he was straining to not climax right at that second. Now I had the upper hand. I began to writhe and move my body beneath him, enjoying watching him trying to restrain himself. I used all my energy and rolled over taking him with me. Now I was on top of him. This move pushed him deep inside me and I let out a sigh as my body accepted him. Then I began to move up and down on top of him and bounce on the bed. He put his hands on my breasts as they bounced. He pinched my nipples lightly and I titled my head back in ecstasy.

Troy put his hands on my waist and then rolled us over. Now he was on top of me. I knew what this meant. He was going to pound me into climaxing, and I was welcome to it. I spread my thighs apart and put my hands on his back and pulled him toward me. He kissed me while lingering inside me.

He pulled away from me and looked deep into my eyes and said it again, "Olivia."

He let out a little sigh and kissed me again, then began to slowly penetrate me. Then it got faster and then harder until it was almost unbearable. He moved in out of me so smoothly we felt like one person. With one loud moan I climaxed. He stopped briefly to kiss me, but then kept going. It was his turn. I was now so sensitive; having him inside me was pure ecstasy. This is what love poems are about, this is what life is about, and I now felt it all. He made one long hard thrust inside me and spilled. He moaned loudly and said my name, over and over, "Olivia, Olivia."

Troy collapsed on top of me. He felt so close to me his heartbeat reverberated through my body. The heat from his skin was so intense I felt like I had my own personal heater.

"I didn't know it could be like that. Olivia you're...magic."

I laughed at this and kissed him. He stayed intertwined and fell asleep like this.

Chapter 46

Over the next two days I stayed in bed with him.

We ordered room service for all of our meals and watched movies. It felt like old times and I was on cloud nine. We made love all over the apartment.

We made love in the shower. We made love on the table. We made love on the floor. We made love in the bed. We christened the entire apartment. It was as if nothing had ever come between us.

I had never been so happy in my life. I could get used to this. I could get used to this for the rest of my life. That thought made me happy. As dysfunctional as we would always be, I knew I couldn't live with the alternative, which was living without him. I would rather be with Troy and live on an emotional roller coaster. A normal life just wouldn't work for me if I tried. It was impossible.

A few days later I was leaving work. A dark car pulled up to the curb and Troy opened the door. "Get in," he said.

I smiled and got in. Troy had a surprise for me. We rolled up to the Gramercy Tavern for dinner. I looked at him and was delighted that we were going out. Our relationship had only been taking place in the bedroom thus far, so this was a refreshing change.

We ate a luxurious and expensive meal and had lighthearted conversation. He would pause and stare at me with his beautiful brown eyes, and my heart would melt.

After dinner we went to Central Park. There he hired a carriage to take us around on a romantic ride around the park. I always thought of this as a cliché tourist thing to do, but I really enjoyed it. We kissed and held hand and hugged to keep each other warm. I loved it.

"I need to tell you something," he said as he looked at me.

"Okay," I said.

"I love you."

I smiled and looked deep into his eyes, unable to believe what I was hearing. It was everything I'd every wanted. I kissed him passionately. "I feel the same way. I love you Troy."

He squeezed my hand and kissed it. Then he pulled me close to him as we looked out at the tall trees of Central Park as we rode in the carriage. I sighed in relief. I felt a weight lifted from me. Hearing his say those words felt like we were creating something real. We were creating something concrete. It felt right, and it felt good.

After the carriage ride we continued being tourists in our own city and went to the top of the Empire State Building. I had only been up here once and that was years ago. I had never been up here with someone that loved me and the experience was completely different. I looked out over the city and all the twinkling lights. How much my life had changed since I met this man was mind blowing. I looked at him and put my hands on his chest. His body was warm and strong.

"You know. I don't even know what you do. For work I mean," I said in amusement. After all this time Troy was still a mystery to me.

He laughed and said, "You don't?"

"No, you're such a mystery to me. After all this time you are still my mysterious Manhattan man," I said.

"I'm in investments, hedge funds and such."

"Oh, I see. I don't really know that means, but okay." I laughed and kissed him.

He stood behind me and hugged me. I loved this new us. It was intoxicating.

Chapter 47

We spent the next week like this. Going out on the town and being a real couple. It made me feel like there was hope for us yet.

Now, I sat on the couch in his apartment scrolling through a magazine. He came out of the bedroom and said, "I hope you don't mind but I ordered room service for us."

"Of course I don't mind. I am hungry too," I said.

This had become our regular routine. He smiled at me and said, "You look beautiful sitting there. I like seeing you in my apartment."

"Thank you, I like being here."

He grinned at me and then came to the couch and laid down. He rested his head on my lap. I stroked his hair with my fingers. He moaned.

A few minutes later there was a knock at the door. Troy opened the door and let the guy roll the cart in. He thanked him and sent him out the door. The cart was little unusual this time. There was a small silver candelabra that had two lit white candles in it. There were two silver domed trays and a pot of coffee. He rolled it over to the couch in front of me.

He poured me a cup of coffee and handed it to me. I smiled at him. This was the hardest part for me. It was spending time together like this that made me feel confused. Was he just using me for my company? I felt like an old married couple when he treated me like this, but I was always on my toes expecting him to disappear. It was an unnerving experience.

After dinner we had a few glasses of champagne. He stared at me, making me feel like I could melt. "Are you happy?" he asked me.

"Yes," I answered.

He leaned in and kissed me. A kiss that immediately lit a fire.

He pulled me close to him and ran his strong hands down the length of my back. I let out a soft whimper and a sigh. He picked me up and cradled me in arms and led me to the bed. Troy was sensual and gentle. He placed me down on the bed and looked down at me. I felt desirable. He caressed my hair, then my face, and let his hands run down to my breasts and cupped them. I was beyond excited. My nipples were hard through my silk dress and Troy ran his hands lightly over them. His hands brushed just the tips of them, and it was exhilarating.

Troy pulled his shirt off over his head revealing a strong hard stomach and smooth skin. He unzipped his pants and pulled them off. Now he lay before me completely naked, and was rock hard. He climbed on top of me and used his strong hands to part my thighs. I moaned with delight. He kissed me softly and then opened my mouth with his tongue. It was a long passionate kiss and I couldn't stop thinking about how right and comfortable this felt, but much more about how I needed this. He pulled my dress over my head and sighed when he saw my naked body.

"Olivia, you are beautiful woman. My woman. I want you."

"I want you too."

He put his mouth around my breast and I was in heaven. He ran kisses down my belly and put his hands under my back holding me up as he explored me. He rolled me over onto my stomach and delicately trailed kisses down the length of my back all the way down and over my buttocks. He massaged it with his hands and it became a mix of a sexual rub down and a deep massage. It was making my entire body tingle with delight. He ran his hands through my long brown hair and rubbed his face against it. Then he moved down to the back of my thighs and placed soft kisses there. He used his tongue to lick a path from my thighs to the back of my knees. He was really enjoying my body.

He rolled me back onto my stomach and placed his body on top of mine.

He looked up and locked eyes with me and with one gentle thrust forward he entered me. He let out a moan and I opened my legs wider to let more of him in. In and out he was slowly thrusting his hips. Moving skillfully and slowly. Then he started uttering some things under his breath about me. I had no clear idea what he was saying, but it seemed so beautiful and romantic I didn't care. I wanted to hear more and more. I arched up to meet him. He pulled out of me and rolled me onto my side. He positioned himself on his side behind me. He entered me again in this position. He put his mouth near my ear and continued to speak to me kissing my neck. His hand was on my waist to steady me as he moved in and out of me. It was incredibly erotic.

Then his whole body tensed up but he restrained himself and stopped. Finally the urge to come passed him and he kept going, but now it was my turn. He reached around with his hand and massaged my breast. It was enough to make me feel over excited. Then his hand trailed down my belly and onto my clitoris. He massaged it all the while still inside me. I tensed up and my breath caught in my throat. That was it; I had an orgasm in this position. Troy slowed his movement as I came. Then he moved faster and faster. He pulled away from me a little and looked down, watching himself go in and out of me. This is what drove him over the edge. With one final thrust he came.

We stayed in this position as he kissed the side of my body. I was in a vortex of ecstasy. I think my body was in a state of shock.

A week went by of feeling blissful. I didn't think that being together would feel this good, but it did. It was such a strong feeling of lust of desire. Troy was mine for now, anyway. It was intense.

"We should go back to the house in Tarrytown," he said one morning a few days later.

I hesitated to answer. I didn't want to go back there. It held some bad memories that I really didn't want to revisit. "I don't know. Work has really picked up so I'm not sure I will be able to escape."

"Okay, well I do have some things I need to take care of and I need to check in with the foreman. I try to go once a month at least. If you can't go this time, you can stay here and I'll be back in a day or two?"

"That sounds like a perfect plan. I would love to stay here and lounge around when I'm not working." I said smiling. I was happy that I was able to get out of not going with ease.

The next morning he left and I invited Lily over to the Plaza for a little room service lunch. I had not seen her for a few weeks. We drank mimosas and had lunch. I told her in detail everything that had been happening. It was a fun couple of days hanging out with my girlfriend. It was a much-needed rest from the emotional roller-coaster I had been riding with Troy.

But it was a break that wouldn't last long. I knew one day that what I had done with Will would come back to haunt me, I just didn't know it would be so soon.

Chapter 48

Two days later I was in a deep sleep in Troy's bed, when I was rudely shaken awake.

"Wake up," he yelled at me.

I was in a haze of sleep, and didn't know what was going on, "What?" I said in a soft tone. I sat up in bed to see Troy pacing the room. He was clearly frazzled and angry.

"Troy? You're back. I missed you."

"Shut up," he barked.

This woke me up. I looked at him and furrowed my brow. "What is it?"

He paced the room some more and then left into the seating area. He came back with the bottle of brandy in his hand. He took giant swigs from it. I was worried and scared. What the hell was happening?

"Did you fuck him?" he asked.

"What? Who? What are you talking about?"

"My brother! You fucked him, didn't you?"

I froze. My eyes opened wide and I fumbled to find the right words to say. Nothing came out.

"I was told by the foreman that he saw Will there more than once while you were still there!" he yelled at me. "That Will was even there early in the morning one day after having spent the night." He threw the bottle across the room.

"Troy, I..."

"Do you deny it?!"

I was silent. I didn't know how to tell him about everything that had happened. I had not had sex with Will, but we had done some things before I had changed my mind. I didn't think that would matter to Troy though.

"It's not what you think," I barely got the words out of my mouth. I felt weak and nauseous.

"Lies!" he yelled. "I want you out of here when I get back. I never want to see you again," he stormed out of the apartment. I called out to him. He left anyway.

Just like that, my dreams were shattered. I didn't know if I could make this right. This was it.

It was over, again.

I remained on the bed with the white silk sheet wrapped tightly around my body. Using it as a security blanket. I needed to hold on to something.

Troy had just stormed out, accusing me of having sex with Will.

An accusation that was only partly true, but I didn't know how to tell him that.

In the moment I couldn't even speak. He had stormed into the apartment like a bull. The energy was intense and he was yelling and raving like a madman. It took me a while to process what was happening when he was yelling. I only felt confused and scared. Then once I realized, I couldn't find the right words to use to tell him what had happened.

How could I tell him that now? We had finally reached a milestone of being happy together. This was a miraculous achievement after all that we had been through. Now I had to try to convince him that what had happened with his brother meant nothing.

I couldn't even bring Lily in on this and have her explain to Troy that she was the reason Will spent the night at the house. I couldn't do that without also exposing what I had actually done with Will before that.

I didn't know if I wanted her to know that.

I heard the elevator bell ring in the distance. He was going to leave me forever, and never look back. I had to catch him. I couldn't lose him again.

With sheer determination and complete foolishness I grabbed the white silk sheets and wrapped them tighter around me. I ran into the sitting room and swung open the front door. I looked down the hallway at the elevator as the doors closed. I couldn't see who was inside. I ran down the hall to the elevator and frantically pushed the button over and over. I pushed the button hoping the doors would open and Troy would be inside. But the doors did not open. I looked around frantically for a way to reach him.

I ran to the end of the hallway and to the stairwell. I swung open the heavy emergency exit door and flew down the stairs. I was focused and determined to stop him from leaving. I grabbed the sheets tighter lifting them so that I didn't trip down the stairs. I ran faster and faster. There were so many flights of stairs and I quickly grew tired. I clearly didn't think this through. I needed to catch him though as it was the most important thing I could think of. I finally reached the bottom of the stairs and exploded into the lobby with a look of fear on my face.

I turned every which way looking for Troy. The lobby was full of people who all stopped and stared at me, but I didn't care. I needed to find Troy. I ran out through the front and onto the outside front steps. I looked at all the cars waiting for passengers from the hotel. I frantically looked for him. Was he in one of these cars? "Troy!" I yelled out. This caught everyone's attention.

The doorman came up to me, "Ma'am, are you alright? Ma'am?"

I ignored him and kept searching. I knew I must look like a wild woman and a crazy one, but I didn't care. The only thing that mattered was getting Troy and bringing him back upstairs with me.

The doorman grabbed my arms tightly, "Ma'am I must insist that you go back to your room. You are making a scene."

I finally stopped and looked at the doorman. I mean really looked at him and looked at his eyes. His face said that he pitied me but was also fearful for his job if he didn't take care of this situation. By situation I mean, my crazy and irrational behavior. I turned. I looked at all the people around me who were completely stopped in their tracks. The hotel guests, visitors, and patrons of the hotel were all looking at me. The pedestrians on the sidewalk glanced over and stared at me, but they didn't stop walking as New Yorkers are always rushing to their destination. I felt a wave of sadness come over me.

A look of defeat swept across my face and I suddenly felt embarrassed and ashamed. I turned back to the doorman who still held my arm. I looked down at my body wrapped in the silk sheets and remembered I was completely naked. I wanted to flee the scene as soon as I possibly could.

"I'm sorry. Yes, I am fine. I'm sorry. Could you help me back to my apartment," I asked the doorman.

"Yes, of course ma'am. Let's go now," the nice old doorman said helping me back inside. We walked fast through the lobby to the elevators. I hung my head low the entire time as I didn't want to make eye contact with anyone. I felt very dumb and knew my behavior was enough to possibly get me arrested.

The doorman was nice enough to clear the elevator and made sure no one else rode with us. As soon as the doors closed tears rolled down my face and I cried. I felt like an idiot. How could I let one man ruin me and who I was? Who exactly was I? I didn't know anymore. The old Olivia would never have put on a scene like I had just done. Yet, here I was doing just that. Is this what love did to people? It made them crazy.

The elevator doors opened once again and the doorman walked me back into the apartment. I had left the door wide open in my haste to catch Troy. I thanked the doorman for his kindness and apologized a thousand times through my tears. Then I closed the door. I collapsed on the bed and didn't move for hours. Now I was trapped here. I couldn't exactly show my face downstairs again. Not after the scene that I had made. I was a complete fool. I curled up on the bed and ran through everything that Troy had said to me. I needed to know more. I needed answers.

Exactly what had happened when he went back to the house? I thought to myself. Had Will confronted him? Had he told him what we did in the library? Or was he merely going off rumors? Maybe he went to the pub and the bartender told him how Lily and I had left with him that night. After all, Tarrytown was a small place and I'm sure everyone knew everyone and I'm positive that the whole town liked to know the latest about the very rich and eligible bachelors that were the Lane brothers. All kinds of ideas started to swirl about in my head. I was making myself sick with worry. Then I decided I would make a stand in this. Troy yelled at me that I needed to be gone from this apartment when he got back. The key words that played over and over in my mind were, "when he got back." That meant he was coming back here to the apartment at some point. I decided then and there that I would not be leaving the apartment. I would stay here until he got back and then I would tell him everything. I knew he wouldn't like it, but I would have to do it.

I suddenly felt better knowing I would indeed see him again. All I had to do was stay here. I just wouldn't leave the apartment. This was his home and he would have to come back to it. Of course I assumed he would be back in the next day or two, and I wouldn't have to wait too long. I wanted to stay with Troy. I wanted to only be with him from this day onward for the rest of my life. I hated myself for not confessing earlier about what had happened with Will, maybe things would be different if I had. We would already be over that obstacle and Troy would be lying here at my side.

That thought was enough to drive me insane.

Chapter 49

I stayed in bed for hours and then I cried myself to sleep that night. In the early morning hours I awoke to strong arms around me.

It was dark and hazy and it felt like a dream. He was back, Troy was back and he was touching me. It was a good sign. I wanted him to want to touch me, to not be able to live without me. I had imagined this moment the entire night before I fell asleep. I had imagined that he would come back to me and forgive me.

I opened my mouth to speak but he silenced me with a "shhh," and put his finger up to my lips. He was right I didn't want to spoil this moment by trying to explain myself. He brushed his lips softly on top of mine. Then brushed his lips on my cheek and down my chin to my neck. My whole body felt alive with his touch. My skin was searing hot under his touch and I had chills running through me. His tongue swept across my neck and down to the tops of my breast. He lightly trailed his tongue on them and slowly made his way to my nipple. He pursed his lips together and grabbed the tip of my nipple in his mouth. He lightly tugged on it and then pressed his tongue flat against it. I closed my eyes and moaned and enjoyed his sensual and slow movements. He kissed and massaged my breasts over and over and then kissed me on the mouth once more. I wanted to tell him, "I love you Troy," but the words wouldn't come out. I couldn't talk.

He trailed kisses all along my inner thighs and then tasted my wetness. He moaned with delight again at how wet he could make me. I raised my leg and propped it on his shoulder. His tongue lightly pressed against my clitoris with burst of pressure. Then he sucked on it gently. A strong vibrational force melted with us and I had the man of my dreams between my legs.

This was now my reality. All this hit me like a truck as Troy continued to lick me. He ate me out for what seemed like half an hour. Every time I was on the brink of climax he would stop and pull away, he enjoyed keeping me on that fine line. Making me beg with my eyes.

He put the tip of his tongue inside me and used his thumb to massage my rose bud. He gently did this, and then it escalated faster and with more pressure. I bit my lip and put my hands in his hair. I couldn't hold on any longer and I came into his mouth.

Troy's muscular body radiated heat, to the point where it seemed like steam was coming off his skin. He climbed on top of me and put the tip of his cock inside me, teased me a little. Our eyes locked as he hovered on top of me. My eyes watered over. The magic of it all was creating a vortex of emotions stronger than anything my body could hold in. His eyes softened as he noticed this in me, he was compassionate and caressed my face. He grabbed my hand and held it as he pushed himself further into me. We were connected. I spread my legs open wider wanting to receive as much of him as I could. I arched my back up letting him go deeper inside me. This is where he paused, and looked directly at me.

Troy concentrated all of his efforts and energy and moved his shaft in and out of me. We moved in perfect rhythm with each other. He softly put his mouth around my breast and squeezed my hand. His tongue circled around the outside of my nipple. All my senses were being stimulated. The magnetic energy or our bodies made me even more sensitive to touch.

I begAn to shake as I neared the heights leading to climax. I moaned louder and writhed under his weight. I couldn't take it anymore. I exploded in ecstasy and yelled out. A yell that seemed to echo across the room and bounce off the walls surrounding us. I relaxed and breathed heavily, but Troy wasn't done.

He stopped, paused and looked deep into my eyes and smiled. I smiled in return. I was filled with joy. Then he continued, moving slowly and leisurely in and out of me. I was extremely sensitive at this point, but it was bearable. I bit my lower lip at the feeling and sensations with every move he made. Now he was moving faster, pumping hard. I opened my legs wide, allowing him to move even faster as he penetrated me. Pounded me. It was happening again. I was reaching orgasm. His face changed and I could tell he was almost there too. I got there first again. My whole body shook. Then with two final thrusts he exploded. It was suddenly silent and still, but the energy was buzzing past us. It was swirling. I could almost see it.

Then a loud buzz went off. I opened my eyes and sat straight up in bed. I was dreaming. It had all been a dream. I leaned over and turned the alarm off. I snapped out of my haze and jumped out of bed. Was he back? Was Troy back? Did I really just dream that? It couldn't be, it was too real. I went into the sitting area and it was empty. I went into the large luxurious bathroom and it was empty. I sat down on the floor and caught my breath. My heart was still racing from my steamy dream.

A few hours later I needed to make a decision. Was I going to go through with this plan to occupy Troy's apartment until he came back? Or would I leave and go home and go on with my life? Staying at the apartment made me feel desperate, and it was humbling. But I couldn't stand the thought of leaving and never seeing him again. Since I didn't have a key to this place I really couldn't come and go as I pleased. Not to mention I didn't want to spend much time walking through the lobby of the hotel after the scene I made last night.

I thought long and hard and weighed the pros and cons of it all. Then I picked up the phone and called work. The receptionist answered and I faked a cold. I told her that I was very ill and very contagious and wouldn't be in for a few days. She encouraged me to get better and that things were fairly quite that day anyway. I hung up the phone and realized that work had become less and less important to me in my life. It was a thought that scared me. What would I do with myself if work were not fulfilling to me anymore? Would I have to go through the pains of a career change and a heavy break up at the same time? That was too much to think about and I forced myself to focus on the present.

When I was done with my work call. I picked up the line and ordered breakfast. I had to admit I had become increasingly addicted to this room service luxury. I ordered a large breakfast and newspaper. I was going to have to settle in the apartment for now. I needed to eat and I needed to occupy myself.

The meal came and the I had I rolled over to the table by the large window.

I drank my hot coffee and scarfed down my meal. It was a hearty Mexican breakfast of huevos rancheros, an egg dish of diced peppers and salsa. It came with a side Spanish rice and strips of sautéed cactus. There was a small bowl with a colorful towel that wrapped around several warm thick corn tortillas. It was delicious and just what I needed to get my day going. Not that I had planned a strenuous day. I only wanted to do relaxing things that felt like treats. I was here to do nothing, but wait.

I relaxed with my feet up on some pillows staring out at the view of New York and read the paper. It was nice to be distracted by what was going on in the world. I had spent so much time and energy in my little bubble of a world that I hadn't paid much attention to the outside world.

Two hours later there was a knock at the door. Who could that be? I thought. If it were Troy he wouldn't knock. I went to the door to see the maid from the hotel. I opened it and she asked if I would like the weekly cleaning. I let her in and she went about doing her job. I did feel strange being in his apartment like this. It was as if I could feel that she knew I wasn't supposed to be there. I tried to not overthink this and went back to reading the paper.

After she left the place was spotless and looked elegant again. It added a sunny brightness to it that I was not seeing before in my blue state of emotions. I put on a movie and continued to wait for Troy. I waited and waited. I watched the door intently. Every time I heard the door of another apartment open my heart skipped. I always thought it was him unlocking the door, but it never was. He never came. Before I knew it the sun was setting and I began to feel disillusioned. Then I jumped as the phone rang. It was the only activity in the apartment for the last few hours so it startled me. I answered it. "Hello?"

There was no answer on the other end. It was just like the mysterious phone call at the house before. Then there was just dial tone. It must be Troy. I pinched myself for picking up the phone. Now that he knew I was still here he definitely wouldn't come back. I needed to do something. I didn't know what.

I decided I would call Lily. I needed to tell her everything. She would probably scold me, but I needed to talk to someone. I needed to know what to do. I was at a lost and felt so alone. I picked up the phone and called her and begged her to come to the apartment. She was already in for the night and didn't want to leave the comfort of her home, but I told her it was of utmost importance.

"Please it's absolutely important and is life changing. Plus there's something I have to tell you."

"But, Olivia it's so late already and I'm already in my pajamas."

"I know, I'm so sorry. I would come to you, but I can't leave the apartment. Something you will understand if I explain it to you. It's a bit wild and crazy and desperate but it is what it is. Will you please, please, please, come?"

"You can't leave the apartment?"

I laughed out loud. I guess it did sound a bit ridiculous. "Yes, I know it sounds strange, but just come please."

"Oh, alright but there better be pizza and wine waiting for me when I get there," she said.

"Done," I said.

We hung up the phone and I ordered a very large New York style pepperoni pizza from an authentic pizza place. The kind of place that was serious about pizza. It arrived about forty-five minutes later, and Lily arrived about ten minutes later. Perfect timing.

I opened a bottle of wine and we curled up on the couch eating our greasy feast. We made a bit of light talk and basic things to catch up, and then I began to pour my heart out.

Chapter 50

"I have a lot to say. Please don't judge me and don't say anything until I'm done," I said.

"Okay, that sounds very serious. I'm ready," Lily said, filling up her glass of wine.

"Troy left. He left me. He's angry with me and he told me to leave the apartment. That was a few days ago. I'm refusing and want a chance to explain myself so I'm staying here until he shows up."

Lily's eyes opened wide and she shifted in her seat. "That is not what I was expecting to hear. So what happened?" she asked.

"I'm not entirely sure. He left for a few days to go to the house in Tarrytown, and when he got back everything changed. You see he accused me of having sex with his brother."

"Oh my god! That is insane. Did you tell him the truth? Did you tell him it was me and not you with Will? How did he even find out?" she asked panicking.

"I assume he found out Will was there that morning. I didn't even get a chance to tell him that he was with you. He wouldn't listen. He was in a crazy rage and left here before I could speak."

"Well, that is awful and I'm sorry I caused trouble. But it seems easy enough to clear up. I'll even speak to Troy if you like and tell him it was me. Once that's cleared up things should go back to normal. It's just a case of mistaken identity. It happens."

"You see, that would help, but that's only part of it." I said closing my eyes and my face turning red.

She gasped, "Did you sleep with Will?"

There was silence. "Well, okay so he does have reason to hate you. I don't blame you - that man is hard to say no to. He is attractive and charming and he knows how to seduce a woman. When did it happen?"

"Well, it didn't actually happen. That's what will be hard to explain to Troy. Will did come to the house when I was alone. It was a time when Troy and I were fighting and I thought it was over. Will caught me in a drunken weak moment. I hated Troy and I wanted to hurt him. I let him kiss me and I let him touch me, and then I came to my senses and kicked him out."

"Touch you?" she queried.

"I stopped it and I didn't have sex with him. Though I'm not sure if Troy will care. But that's not all."

"What else?" she asked, but luckily she didn't seem hurt or annoyed about my history with Will.

"Before that happened, he hit on me at a wedding. I went with Troy and he introduced me to the family. I got drunk and Will cornered me in the hall and started with his seduction routine. He was saying all the things he says and coming on strong. I got lost in it, but I did back away ... eventually. But Troy saw it. They fought and punched each other. It was a mess. So you see there was already history. I don't know why they hate each other. Troy mentioned that Will always tried to steal his girlfriends and usually succeeded. So there's that."

Lily was silent. She filled her glass again and then filled mine. Then after a few moments she said, "What are you going to do?"

"I don't know. I'm so lost. That's why I brought you here. I need help. Tell me what to do."

"I can't make that call, only you can," she said.

"Well, what would you do?" I asked her.

She pondered for a while and picked up another slice of pizza. She ate and was silent. Finally she said, "You want Troy back?"

"Yes, he's the one. I don't want to be without him. I can't be."

"Then you have to tell him the truth. Everything. It will hurt him but he's already hurting. He might not want you after that.

But that's something you will have to deal with. At least the truth will be out and over with."

She was right. I had to tell him what I let Will do to me.

"You're right."

"So you're just going to stay here? Until he comes back? What about work?" she asked.

"I called in sick. But truthfully I have started to loathe that job. It's not fulfilling for me anymore. Nothing is, except him."

"You sound like a junkie." She laughed a little.

"I know. Love and desire, the ultimate drugs." I said. I sighed and gave her a big hug. "Thanks for the talk. Stay here with me, it's late."

We fell asleep watching movies and I counted myself lucky for having such a great friend.

The next morning we had breakfast and read the paper. I ordered turkey sausages, eggs, and waffles. We topped it all off with freshly squeezed orange juice and coffee. Lily left me with more words of encouragement and promised to call me later to check in on me.

She left early and headed back to her apartment to get ready for work. I settled in to once again wait it out. I wondered how long it would be before cabin fever set in, I thought to myself. I grabbed a pack of cards and played solitaire. I took a long hot bubble bath and lounged around in a plush robe. I watched three movies and then a nature channel documentary. What else could I do with myself, I thought.

After dinner, Lily called to check up on me. It was nice to talk to someone. I listened to her talk about work and general complaints about the subway and traffic.

After we hung up I opened a bottle of wine. If just to pass the time, but before I knew it I was opening another bottle. Later that night I drank myself to sleep. This was becoming an awful habit.

I was startled awake by the loud ring of the telephone. I jumped up out of bed and ran over to it. I was ready to answer it, and then I stopped myself. I knew it was Troy and if I answered he wouldn't come back. I stared at it and just let it ring. After it went silent, I became hopeful. Now maybe he would think I was gone. I felt excited to see him.

I cleaned up the apartment and made it look like I was gone. I turned off all the lights and then went into the bedroom and sat in a chair to await his return. The wine and late night hour slowly took over me and I was soon asleep again.

Chapter 51

About an hour later I felt the warmth of a soft kiss on my lips. I moaned and smiled. It was Troy and he had come back to me. I felt a haziness that I couldn't shake. I wanted to say more. I couldn't move and felt heavy. Then I realized it was another dream. I was still asleep.

I forced myself to stay asleep so that I could at least be with him in my dreams. That was all I could remember from my slumber.

I awoke the next morning to the sound of my piercing alarm once again. I jumped out of the chair and turned it off. That's when I felt the pain in my neck. It was sore from falling asleep in the chair. I couldn't believe I fell asleep in the chair like that. I must have had a lot of wine. I guess I really didn't eat that much of dinner. I had lost my appetite lately.

I walked around the room massaging my neck and my aching head. Then I remembered the phone calls last night. Troy could walk in at any moment and I wanted to be ready. I got up and went to the bathroom to brush my teeth and wipe the sleep from my eyes. I brushed my long brown hair and pulled it into a sleek high pony tail. I made myself presentable.

I walked into the sitting room and noticed something was wrong. Things just looked out of place somehow. I walked around the apartment and then into the large walk in closet. Drawers were open or half closed, and clothes were missing off the hangers. There were many empty spots were shoes would go and other items. I looked for further clues and realized that Troy *had* come in the middle of the night. I was infuriated with myself for falling asleep. I'd missed my chance to talk to him. I'd missed my chance to just see him. And I'd missed my chance to touch him. After all this time I had invested in waiting for him, camping out at his apartment, I had slept through his visit. Now I didn't know what to do.

I remembered the kiss in my sleep. Was that real? Did he still love me? Why didn't he wake me up? Why didn't he shake me awake? Why didn't he yell at me and force me to leave? He could have me escorted out of the building in no time flat, but he didn't. Instead he stole a secret kiss in the middle of the night.

It was all so confusing but that was a good sign. Maybe he still wanted me. It made me feel like we were still in fact together, and just having another rough patch. If you could call what we had been doing as "together." I really didn't know what we had. I had that secret kiss though, and that was a comforting feeling.

I picked up the phone and called Lily. I told her what had happened and we sort of laughed about it. It was absurd that after all I this time of me waiting for him I missed him because I got drunk.

Now I needed another plan. I couldn't stay in this apartment any longer. I needed to take action. Lily suggested that I go to the house in Tarrytown. That he was probably there. I doubted he was there. Why would he want to be in a place that he thinks I had sex with his brother? Then she said something that made sense, "Do you have any other choice?"

She was right. If he had gone anywhere I wouldn't know where to go. With his amount of money he could be anywhere in the world. But I didn't know any of those places. I did however know where the house was. If I went however, I would surely lose my job. I needed to get back to work. I needed to get back to my life, or I could go search for him. I thought long and hard about it, and then I knew exactly what I was going to do. I had made a decision.

I took a hot shower and then got dressed. I looked around the apartment and burned the way it looked into my memory. It was possible I would never be back here again. That thought made my heart ache. I stared at the bed and replayed the memory in my mind of when I first came up to this apartment. That first day that we collided when I spilled coffee on him. I pictured myself standing on the bed, just a shy scared girl. I could almost hear his voice commanding me to do things. It was an intoxicating thought.

I went into the sitting room and imagined us eating room service and watching old movies under a blanket. All these memories only strengthened the fact that this was worth fighting for. We and what we had together was worth fighting for.

I grabbed a pad of paper and wrote, "I love you Troy." I laid it on the pillow. Just in case I didn't find him, I needed him to see this when he finally came back.

I locked the door to the apartment and went downstairs. I walked briskly through the lobby, as I didn't want to be recognized as the crazy woman wrapped in sheets from a few nights before. I walked fast and walked out of the apartment and down the sidewalk.

When I got to my apartment I quickly changed and was on my way. I didn't bother to pack a bag, as I really didn't know what I was in for. It was possible he wasn't at the house and I would be back home in a few hours. Or he could be there and would send me away as soon as he saw me. I tried not to overthink it and left.

Chapter 52

I grabbed a cab to Grand Central Station on 42nd Street. I really never spent much time at this train station and I forgot how massive and beautiful it was. I bought a ticket to Tarrytown at the ticket vending machine and then stopped to look up at the astronomical ceiling.

A few minutes later I was on board the train and feeling nervous. I didn't know what would happen, but it felt right to be doing something instead of just waiting around for something to happen. Once we were out of the city I stared out the window. The trees and plant life gave way to familiar scenery. I missed the look and feel of the countryside. I forgot the effect it had on me.

A flood of memories came back to me. I thought of Troy and I on his yacht lazily flowing up the Hudson River. We really enjoyed ourselves then, before things got so complicated. He opened my eyes to so much by showing me the countryside of the Hudson Valley. I was forever grateful for that. The amount that my life had changed since this man came into my life was beyond measurable. I was now a confident woman, when I used to be fumbling my way through life. I was afraid of being naked and enjoying my body, and that had changed. I had experienced so much. All of this was filling my mind with joy as I sat in the train. It passed small rural farms and the sky was a perfect shade of blue. It was a touching moment, and I didn't realize how much I was now a different person until now. If Troy and I never got back together, than I would at least have had the experience of becoming a brand new woman.

The train stopped at Tarrytown and I disembarked and got into a waiting cab. I was sweating and nervous. My heart and mind wasn't ready to face the wrath of him yelling at me. But it was necessary; he had every right to be angry and to express that anger by yelling. I wasn't looking forward to telling him what I did with Will. I knew it would hurt him, but at least it was a lot less than what he thought really happened.

The cab pulled up to the enormous house and my heart sank. It was beautiful and stunning just as I had remembered, but what really made my stomach ache was the black SUV in the driveway. He was here. Troy was here and now I would have to face the music.

I paid for the cab and walked up the driveway. I half expected him to run out of the front doors and yell at me. Forcing me to leave. But it was extremely silent.

I could hear the crickets chirping and the wind rustling through the leaves. I took in a deep breath and knocked on the door. I fixed my shirt and ran my fingers through my hair. I waited a few seconds. No one came to the door. I knocked louder, after all it was a big house and it would be hard to hear a knock. I balled my fist and pounded loudly on the door. I waited again, but no answer. I turned the knob and to my surprise the door opened. I quietly went inside. I looked around and the house was eerily silent. Where was he? Maybe he was asleep. Then my heart dropped as the thought of him being in bed with another woman made me feel sick. It was not something I wanted to walk in on. But I had come this far and I needed to find him.

I searched the first floor first as it felt less obtrusive. I walked into the kitchen and poured myself a glass of water. I took a little breather and finished the glass. I went into the library and it was empty. I looked at the desk for any signs that he was working from here. I quickly remembered being with Will on the desk. I pushed it out of my mind. He would probably throw the desk away after he knew.

I finally summoned the courage to walk up the stairs. I went slowly and quietly listening for any signs of activities. Especially any signs of sex, but I heard nothing. I went into the master bedroom. I looked around and there were no signs that anyone was in there. I didn't see clothes, or a bag, or shoes. I saw nothing. The bed was made and it was supremely clean. That was odd I thought. Clearly someone was here because the car was outside. I went into the guest bedroom next and was shocked to see all of Troy's stuff. Why was he staying in the guest bedroom? That was the oddest thing. I went to a shirt that was laid on the bed and picked it up. I held it close to me and rubbed it on my face. I inhaled his scent. It was intoxicating and I had to fight back tears. I loved him. I did. I really loved him. The fact that a shirt could have this effect on me proved that. I went to the window and looked out over the grounds. Where was he? I needed him. I needed his presence near me. I needed to see him and hear his voice.

I walked the long path to the stables only to find that it too was empty. I came back out and stood in the grass staring at the house.

I looked out over the tree tops and remembered the trails. I remembered how he had shown me all of his favorite places. Then I knew exactly where he was. He had to be at the overlook where we once hiked to and made love.

I put the shirt down and readied myself for a little hike. I grabbed some paper and left a note for him. "I'm here. I went searching for you on the trails. I love you." I left the note on his pillow. I grabbed some water and headed out the door.

I found the trail head that went up to the overlook and started walking. I thought about what I would say to him when I saw him. I practiced my speech. I knew he would be mad at me so I would let him get that steam out first. Then I would say my piece. I would tell him about Lily and Will and I would tell him about what happened in the library.

I came to a fork in the road. I looked both ways. I didn't remember this part of the trail. Troy had always led and I just sort of followed. I never really paid that close attention. One trail looked like it climbed higher so I chose that one. I continued on my way. I looked up at the trees and marveled at their beauty. I truly loved it here. It was very peaceful and wild. The forest had an old world charm to it that I couldn't describe in words. It was just an energy and a feeling. I climbed higher and the trail got steeper. My thighs started to burn and I needed to stop to take a breather. I didn't remember this trail being that strenuous but I was probably just out of shape from sitting in Troy's apartment for days doing nothing. I thought about how he had come in when I was sleeping on the chair in the middle of the night and kissed me. That was a hopeful sign. I smiled at the thought of him not being able to not touch me that night. This thought made me continue hiking to look for him. I needed to get to the overlook and be with him and to talk to him.

I walked and walked and climbed higher and higher, then the trail did something odd, it dipped and went down. It was now leading into the canyon. That's odd, I thought. I don't think this is the right way. I turned and looked around and saw another trail in the distance. That was why this trail was going into the canyon. I was on the wrong trail. I crossed through the brush going off the trail I was on now and made my way to the other trail. I felt so stupid. I was so lost in my thoughts and practicing my speech of what I would say to Troy that I didn't realize I was on the wrong trail. How long had I been walking anyway? I reached the new trail and began to follow it up. I knew the overlook was high up on the edge of a cliff so I needed to go up.

An hour later I still had not reached the overlook. I looked around confused. I looked up at the sun for some sort of direction and realized it was already setting. How was it already sunset? I started to panic. I was lost. I turned in my tracks and started retracing my steps. It was fine. I would just go back the way I came. Or so I thought. More time passed and I couldn't find the other trail that I had originally started on. It was now twilight and it would be pitch black in an hour or less. I had already drunk the last of the water I brought with me, and I was very thirsty. I was glad it was not hot, but the temperature was dropping fast. It would be very cold over night. I wondered if Troy had made it back to the house. Did he see my note? What he never went back to the house for several days? So many thoughts ran through my mind. I was terrified. Would this be the end of me? What kinds of animals were out here? Bears, cougars, I really had no idea. I had to make a decision. Either I would stop and wait to be found or keep wandering around trying to find my own way out. If I stopped I ran the risk that no one was looking for me at all. I would just be stuck here. Plus walking kept me warm. Or if someone was looking for me, then I made it a lot harder for them to find me by wandering around the woods. I could be go further away from the house for all I knew. I racked my brain wondering what I should do. I needed to make a decision. It was such a change that a few hours ago I was looking for Troy, and now I hoped he was looking for me. It could be a life or death situation. I found a large boulder sat on it and began to cry. I cried as quiet as I could, as I didn't want to alert any animals of my presence. I would sit here for a while and if no one came I would keep moving. I felt stupid.

Chapter 53

I don't know how much time had passed, but it felt like hours. It was very dark and I was frightened. Then I heard something in the woods. I began to panic. It sounded like hooves echoing through the forest. My breath caught in my throat. I stood still and the hairs on the back of my neck stood up. Then I heard it, "Olivia? Olivia!"

It was Troy. I almost fainted I was so happy to hear him. I looked around and saw a light in the distance. I yelled out, "Troy! I'm over here!"

"Olivia?"

"Yes! I'm here!" I cried. Tears of joy and happiness overwhelmed me.

"I can't see you. Keep calling, I'll find you," he shouted.

I called out to him again and again as he came closer. Suddenly he came through the brush on top of a horse. He was holding a flashlight and had a rifle strapped to his back. He saw me and jumped off the horse and came to me. He hugged me so tightly I could scarcely breathe.

"Olivia, Olivia," he said over and over. "I thought I'd lost you."

"I'm so sorry. I came to look for you and I got lost. I'm so sorry. I was so scared."

He handed me a bottle of water and made me drink slowly from it.

Then he grabbed my face in his hands and said, "Don't ever do that again. Do you promise me?"

He covered my mouth with his and kissed me. "Come on. Let's go home," he said.

We both got on the horse. I wrapped my arms around his waist and buried my head in his back. I had never felt safer than I did now. His body was warm and I held onto him tightly.

We silently rode through the woods back to the house. I was shocked at what I saw when we came out of the woods. There were several police cars parked in the driveway with their red and blue siren lights on. There was one ambulance and a people standing around with supplies. Was all this for me?

"I called them before I left to find you. I didn't know what I would find or if I would need help."

"Thank you," I said and squeezed him tighter.

We got closer to the small search party that had assembled. I heard voices, and they were relieved to see me. I felt silly for causing so much trouble. But one thing was sure. Troy cared for me. He wouldn't have summoned an entire town to search for me if he didn't.

We approached the front door of the house. Troy carried me off the horse. A paramedic helped him and Troy nodded at me as they sat me in the back of an ambulance. They looked me over, though I assured them that I wasn't hurt. I was just a little shaken up. They shined a light in my eyes, checked my blood pressure and heartbeat. They inspected my limbs for breaks or cuts in my skin. They confirmed that I was dehydrated, but not at a dangerous level. They handed me electrolyte drinks and ordered me to sip on them. I did feel exhausted and a bit light headed, but they assured me this was normal after a traumatic incident like this one. I sat in the back of the ambulance wrapped in a heat blanket until they confirmed I was okay to not go to the hospital. I watched as the search party unassembled.

I could see Troy talking to the sheriff and explaining everything. He was filling out a report. My heart swelled with pride as I watched him. He was all man and I felt safe knowing he was nearby. Finally the sheriff came over to me and asked me what happened. I told him everything and apologized over and over for getting lost and wasting all of their energy and time to be out here. He was kind and was glad that I was okay. It was nice and comforting to know that I would have eventually been rescued even if Troy had not found me.

Finally, they all left the property. It was late and I was so tired. Troy picked me up and carried me inside. He laid me down on the couch and said, "Drink more water. I'm going to put the horse away and I will be right back." He kissed me on the forehead and left.

I drank small sips of water and rehydrated myself. I was still feeling cold so I went upstairs and started a hot bath. I took off all my clothes and submerged myself in it. It was all I could do to stop myself from trembling.

A few minutes later Troy walked in. He was carrying a trey with a few sandwiches and some hot tea. He looked at me and that look came across his face. A lustful look that said he wanted me.

"I'm sorry. I was so cold. I couldn't stop trembling. This was the only way I could think of to warm myself up."

His look changed from lust to concern. "How long were you out there? Should I call a doctor?"

"No, I think I will be fine. I just need to warm up. I'm not exactly sure how long I was out there. Maybe since three o' clock I think."

Troy put the tray down and handed me the hot tea. It was soothing and warmed me on the inside. He grabbed a sponge and started rubbing my body. I closed my eyes and sighed.

His touch was soft and therapeutic. It was exactly what I needed.

He slowly washed me. I looked up at him tears rolled down my face. He wiped them away.

"Don't. We can talk later. Just relax for now. Let the shock leave you. You need to warm up."

"I know what will warm me up more," I said. He smiled and stood up. He took off all his clothes and climbed in the tub with me.

We took in every curve of each other's body. Exploring every inch of it. We kissed and caressed each other. The thought that I could have died out there only made the energy between us thicker. We were bonded. He smiled at me and kissed me. I ran my hands all over his body and reached into the water and put my hands around his cock. Then I straddled him again. I guided him inside me and sat down on top of him to push him in deep.

With him inside me my eyes began to water over a little. I was so full of emotion. I was in love with this man. No, I was deeply and helplessly in love with this man. He pulled me close and ran his hand over my breast. His thumb ran across my hard nipple. Then he put his lips on it, kissing it gently. I was in heaven. I never wanted this to end. I ran my hands through his dark hair. He was a real man, a hero that went out on horseback in the middle of the night into the dark forest to rescue me. After touching and rubbing every inch of him, I began to move up and down on him again. It made the water in the tub move around us in waves. It felt so good against my skin.

When I was about to reach orgasm I slowed down and paced myself. We would have to talk about things eventually. He would hate me for what I did with Will. This could be the last time he was inside me. I held him close and kissed his neck. Then I buried my face in his chest. I never wanted to leave this moment. Troy put his arms around me and sighted and said, "It's okay. You're okay now. It's over."

He kissed me and I started moving again. Up and down. He grabbed onto my hips and guided me. Then we both reached orgasm. I yelled out in ecstasy.

We stayed entwined in the tub. Then Troy got out and grabbed a towel. I stood up and he wrapped it around me. He carried me out of the tub and into the bed. I stretched out and tried to keep my eyes open. I wanted to talk to him. I wanted to tell him that I had not had sex with Will, but I was so tired. Hours and hours of walking around the forest and then the emotional trauma of being lost in the woods had got the best of me. I dozed off to sleep.

Chapter 54

The next morning I awoke to an empty bed. It felt awful. Though it did look like Troy had slept next to me.

I searched around instinctively for a note. I didn't want to find one, but I knew it was a sure sign that he had left me yet again. I began to panic not knowing if he would feel different about me today. Had he got over the trauma of last night and remembered that he was angry with me?

Then I heard the clanging of pots from downstairs and smelled the aroma of coffee. I smiled. He was here and he was in the kitchen. I felt relieved, very happy, and extremely excited. I brushed my hair and brushed my teeth. I took care to freshen up as much as I could. I didn't bring anything with me from home and my clothes were dirty from being in the woods. I put on a robe and went downstairs.

I stood in the doorway to the kitchen. He was thoroughly involved and focused on cooking. I was having fun watching him cook. He didn't notice my presence and it felt good to watch him smile as he took care of me. My heart warmed in response. I finally spoke up, "Smells good."

He stopped and looked at me and that brilliant grin lit up his face.

"You didn't eat last night so I figured you would be very hungry."

"I am thank you."

"You gave me quite a scare yesterday."

"I know. I'm sorry. I didn't mean to, but I really did think I was going to die out there. So thank you. Thank you for coming to look for me."

He came over to me and put a plate down in front of me and kissed me on the forehead. The plate was full of scrambled eggs, bacon, and potatoes. A plate of toast with butter next to it was already on the table. Then he brought over another plate with large stack of pancakes on it, and then he set down a bottle of maple syrup. Next he brought a large glass of water over to me and said, "No coffee for you until you've rehydrated."

I smiled and said, "Okay." I ate heartily and he watched me with amusement as I ate. We sat at the table in silence eating and looking at each other. I couldn't stop smiling. I was so happy to be with him. It made me feel giddy.

I didn't know what was happening here. Had the thought of losing me to death really changed over a new leaf for him? I was enjoying this moment with him, but I knew eventually we would have to have the talk.

After breakfast I went upstairs to lay down for a bit while he worked. I stared at myself in the mirror and wondered how I would tell him about Will. The only thing I could think of was to blurt it out. That was really the only way. I knew he wouldn't want to hear it, but the anxiety was killing me. I needed to get it over with.

With determination I went downstairs and looked for him. He was in the library of all places. He sat at his desk going over a few documents.

"Troy, we need to talk. You don't have to say anything, but please just hear me out."

A dark look came over his face. I could tell he didn't want to hear it.

"Please?" I said.

He crossed his arms over his chest and stared at me. Then he finally nodded.

"I never had sex with your brother."

"I don't want to hear it," he said through tight lips.

"Please just listen. He was here and he stayed the night, but he was here with my friend, Lily. After you left she came up to visit me. I couldn't be alone. We went to a pub, the Horsefeathers and he was there. They got along and he came back here with us. He stayed with her in the guest room."

He raised his eyebrows at me. He knew that wasn't the end of it.

"But that's not all. I never had sex with your brother. But he did try that night, after you left. We did some ... things, but then I kicked him out."

A murderous look came across his face. I immediately stepped back and felt scared.

"Tell me."

I swallowed hard and took a deep breath. "You have to understand. After you left that note, I was a mess. I got really drunk. I tore this room apart. The library. I threw everything out of the drawers. I'm sure you noticed that. Then I collapsed on the mess I made. I heard the door open and I thought it was you. It was Will. He had let himself in."

Troy was clenching his fists now. I wasn't sure how much more he would listen to.

"Go on," he said.

"I was so drunk. I thought it was over. I thought you never wanted to see me again. He came in and I yelled at him for causing so much pain between us. I went up to him and slapped him. Then he caught my hand and kissed it. He said so many things. Things that felt comforting and I needed that in that moment. I was so alone and heart broken. Then it got out of hand. He kissed me, and I kissed him back. He picked me up and carried me to the desk. But that's when I stopped him and came to my senses. I forced him to leave. And that's it."

Troy's eyes narrowed. He stood up and picked up the chair and flung it across the room. My eyes opened wide and I was terrified. But I was expecting this. Of course he would be mad. I had to tell him everything. I didn't want to leave out too many details, because it would haunt me forever. I started to cry. "I'm so sorry Troy. But I thought you had left me. I thought it was over."

Troy cleared the desk with one arm throwing everything off of it. He grabbed at his hair and then looked at me. Tears were in his eyes. He stared at me and then took steps toward me. I stepped back, but he blew right past me. He ran out the front door and yelled, "I'll kill him."

"No. Don't go. It meant nothing!" I cried after him.

A few moments later the tires squealed on the driveway as he left.

Chapter 55

I paced up and down the house. I was so worried. I didn't know where Troy had gone, and I didn't know what he was capable of. I couldn't stand not knowing.

Hours went by and he never returned.

I sat by the window staring out at the driveway. Night had fallen and he still was not back. Then I saw lights coming down the driveway. I stood up and felt hopeful. I was excited and scared all at once. As the car got closer I realized it wasn't the black SUV I was used to seeing. It was a car. Who could that be?

My question was soon answered as Troy's mother stepped out of the car. I went straight to the door and let her in. She looked exhausted and it scared me even more. What had Troy done?

"What's happened? Where's Troy? Is he okay?"

"He's in jail."

I froze. Oh, no he must have done something to Will. "Why what happened? How long is he in jail? Is everything alright?"

"He and his brother got into another fist fight at the pub. Nothing out of the ordinary, and neither of them is extremely hurt. Except for bruised egos I'm sure."

"Oh thank God." I exhaled in relief. It wasn't as bad as I had suspected. I relaxed and let my body go loose for the first time in hours.

"Come let's have some tea. There is much to talk about."

I followed Tabitha into the kitchen and made tea. She sat down and began to tell me a long story. I was shocked by it. She told me about how Troy and Will had never been able to get along. They always fought over everything. Then she told me the most shocking thing. I never thought of it at all, but they weren't just brothers, they were twins. My mouth dropped open.

"Twins?" I said in shock.

"Yes. I assumed you didn't know because neither of them likes to admit it. They are not identical obviously, but they are fraternal twins. Raising them has been the hardest thing."

I stood up from my chair. Suddenly everything made sense. It was so clear now. This fight between the two of them had been raging since birth. Now I understood why I also found Will so attractive.

"It's always been a problem?" I said.

"Oh yes, always. Since they were boys, they would fight over toys. They could never share and it was because they were so alike. Then as they got older fighting over toys turned into fighting over girls."

"I see."

"I don't know if it will ever stop. Once I thought it would if either of them married, then the other would respect that. Susannah was promised once to Troy and then Will ended up having his way with her and ended that."

"Susannah."

"Yes, I believe you met her before."

"Yes, I did. I didn't know what had happened though."

"When Troy showed up with you, I hoped it would all be over. He hasn't introduced a woman to the family in a very long time. I assume because he fears his brother's actions. Will has also not introduced us to a girlfriend because of the same fear. Troy has also ... had his way with Will's girlfriends."

I suddenly felt relieved. The fact that Troy had seduced Will's girlfriends would have to make him sympathetic to Will seducing me. It just had to. Turns out I was beating myself up over nothing. All along I was just a toy they were fighting over. I knew that Troy loved me, but this whole thing with his brother was just that. It was a thing with his brother. I just happened to get caught in the crossfire.

"Thank you. I didn't know any of this and it makes me feel less confused."

"I figured someone should tell you. I knew Troy never would. He hates talking about it."

"So now what. How long will he be in jail?"

"They are both being bailed out right now. He will probably be home soon. A word of advice - let him cool off for a few hours before engaging him in conversation. I learned that much over all these years."

"Okay I will. Thank you." I gave her a big long warm hug. Then she left. I didn't know what to do with this new information. Twins. That would be why they were so much alike. Even the way they seduced me was so similar. It was what drew me to them in the first place.

After Tabitha left I didn't know what to do with myself. I called Lily and told her everything that had happened. She scolded me for going off in the woods and getting lost. I talked to her for an hour and it was good to get all that information off my chest. She encouraged me to listen to Troy with an open heart and to stop stressing. Just take things one minute at a time. I hung up the phone and felt better. She always helped me feel better.

An hour later Troy walked in. He looked at me. His lip was busted open and he had a black eye. I went up to him and hugged him, but I said nothing. He hugged me back and I was relieved. I led him to the kitchen. I still said nothing. I nursed him as best as I could. I put ice on his lip and a piece of uncooked steak over his eye. We didn't talk for hours.

Later that night I crawled into bed with him. I knew he must be exhausted so I continued with my silence. Talking could wait.

The next morning I awoke before he did. He looked so peaceful even with a bruised face. I whispered, "I love you," in his ear. I kissed his chest and climbed on top of him straddling him like a koala bear and went back to sleep. It felt good to have him beneath me again.

Chapter 56

When he woke up later, he looked at me. I wondered if he had forgiven me. I didn't want to talk about it anymore. I think we had both had enough. He looked at me and said, "Let's get out of here."

"Okay. Where should we go? Back to the city? I'm pretty sure I've lost my job at this point."

"I'm sorry," he said.

"That's okay. I had other important things to see to."

He smiled at me and said, "I have an idea. Let's have breakfast and then we'll leave in a few hours."

"Okay," I said suspiciously. He had that mischievous smile that said he was hiding something. I played along. I didn't care what we did as long as we were together. That's all that mattered to me. I went upstairs and put on some of his clothes. I found a button down shirt that would work and almost fit me like a dress. I put on a pair of his shorts and tied them tight with a belt to keep them from falling off.

We ate a full breakfast and then we closed up the house and left. We drove through the town and came upon the docks. There on the river was his beautiful yacht. The same one we had taken to get to the house the first time we came here. I gasped at the sight of it. It was more beautiful than I remembered. I looked at him and smiled. He winked at me.

We boarded the yacht and set sail down the Hudson back toward New York City. We sat on the deck and watched the farmlands go by. The river seemed to be flowing slower than usual and we were in no rush to get back. Most of the trees had lost their leaves and stark white branches reached high into the sky. I stood up on the deck and walked over to the rail. I inhaled deeply and closed my eyes. I was happy once again. A few moments later strong arms were around me. Troy leaned his body against my back and put his head on my shoulder. Together we stared out at the banks of the river.

"I've been thinking about selling The Plaza apartment," he said.

I opened my eyes wide, "Really? Why?"

"Well it's really not big enough for two people and I kind of want to get a new place where we can start fresh, together."

I smiled at him tilted my head toward him. I kissed him on the cheek and said, "I think it's a good idea. Plus there's no privacy there. I like my privacy."

"You do?"

"Yes, of course."

"Well maybe we should go somewhere private for a while. Somewhere different and new where we can forget the past and make new memories."

"I would really like that. I would go anywhere with you," I said.

"I believe you," he said.

"The way you went into the woods to look for me. That takes a lot of courage. Don't do it again, but it took a lot of courage."

"I won't do that again. I'm sorry."

I turned around and hugged him. He kissed me and we stayed locked that way for a few moments. I was in complete bliss. Troy ran his hands down my back and then began to rub his hands all over me. Soon we were both aroused. He grabbed my hand and kissed it softly.

"Come on," he said.

I followed him inside the yacht and down the corridor into the cabin bedroom.

"Olivia, I still want to be with you. I have fallen for you, more than any other woman I have ever known. Do you feel the same? Be honest please."

My head spun with joy, "Yes."

Troy didn't say anything more. He picked me up in his strong arms and kissed me, and then he threw me on the bed. He put his mouth on mine and let his tongue explore my mouth. I wanted him. I wanted this. I wanted this forever. This was heaven to me.

I breathed heavily as he slowly unbuttoned the buttons on his shirt that I wore and let my breasts free. He moaned at the sight of them. He ran his hands over them and the tips of my nipples were instantly hard. He leaned down and put one in his mouth. I ran my fingers through his hair and grabbed onto it. He ran kisses down my belly and unbuckled the belt I wore. He took of my shorts and then put his hands under my bottom. He squeezed and arched my back up holding me. He rolled me onto my side and softly made a path of kisses down the length of my back. He went over the curve of my hips and down the length of my legs. It was exhilarating. Goosebumps appeared on my body under his light touch. "I love you, Olivia."

"I love you too."

My breathing grew heavier. This was a man that knew a woman's body and he was all mine. He licked and sucked and then added his long fingers to the mix. He inserted two fingers inside me while keeping his mouth attached to my nipples. It was too much! It was the most intense orgasm I've ever had, even to this day. I continued to spasm for what seemed like several minutes. It lasted so long and made my entire body felt alive and tingly. Troy finally moved away. He pulled himself on top of me, grabbed my hand and placed it over his cock. I caressed it softly, and then released it from his pants. He moaned, but he never closed his eyes. We stayed, eyes locked together, me searching for what made him feel really good. I was so wet. I sat up and began to undress him slowly. I loved looking at his body. His rock hard chest and strong arms made me melt. I caressed his body and then peeled his pants off.

He rolled me back onto my back and placed his body on top of mine.

He locked eyes with me and kissed me, then placed himself inside of me and let out a moan. It slipped in so easily, and I heard a heavy breath from him that let me know it felt good. He stayed inside me, not moving for a few seconds while he kissed me.

I opened up wider to let more of him in. He moved deeper inside me.

He massaged my clitoris while moving inside me. I tensed up and then released into an orgasm again, crying out.

We made love again and again that entire day until we arrived back in Manhattan.

Chapter 57

The next day we went to my apartment. I looked around and realized I hadn't been there in a really long time except to stop in and change.

It seemed like a foreign place to me, mostly because Troy did not live here. It was the place that old Olivia lived. The new Olivia was a completely different woman.

Troy sat on my couch and instructed me to pack and bring my passport. I assumed this meant that we were going out of the country, but I didn't question it. I liked that he took pleasure in surprising me. I was up for anything as long as I was with him.

An hour later we were downstairs hailing a cab. We went to JFK airport but we didn't board an international flight as I thought we would. Instead we boarded a plane to Las Vegas.

"Vegas? Why do I need my passport for Vegas?" I asked

"It's just a pit-stop. I have to take care of some things first," he said.

"Okay," I said. Though something in the way he said it didn't really have me convinced.

We sat in first class and drank champagne. Anyone looking at us would think we were on honeymoon. The way we played and teased each other, and the way we paused to stare into each other's eyes was enough to make any cynic think twice. We snuggled under a blanket and watched an inflight movie. I fell asleep from the champagne and he held me tight the entire time.

A few hours later we arrived in Vegas. We took a cab from the airport to the Bellagio hotel. We checked into a luxury suite and then took another nap. A few hours later we took in a show and dinner. We gambled a little and Troy laughed at me as I tried to play cards and roulette. I only won a few times, but it was fun. We laughed and drank and had a good time together. I couldn't figure out whatever business he needed to take care of in Vegas and he wouldn't give me any hints.

I assumed he was meeting a high powered client and didn't bother to ask anymore.

The next day I slept in late. I woke up and Troy was sitting on the bed staring at me.

"I love watching you sleep. You are like a beautiful angel."

"Thank you," I said. I gave him a light kiss on the cheek. I sat up and my hand touched something on the bed. It was a black garment bag.

"What's that?" I asked.

"It's your dress."

I laughed. "A dress?"

He unzipped the bag and opened it. It was a white silk dress. It was long and elegant with lace trim and expensive beading. I gasped and put my hands up to my mouth. Was this what I think it was? There is only one occasion that called for a dress like this one. I looked at him with wide eyes and with my mouth dropped open. "Is that a …? Is that a wedding dress?" I could barely get the words out.

"I didn't bring you here because I had business. I brought you here to marry you. I hope you don't mind but I can't wait anymore. I want you to be my wife, Olivia. If you will have me?"

Tears rolled down my face. I jumped up and hugged him. I couldn't believe this was real. We were really getting married. It was all I had hoped for. It was what I had dreamed of and now it was happening.

"Yes!" I screamed. "A thousand times yes! When? How long do I have to get ready?"

He laughed, "A couple of hours. Can you do it?"

"Yes!"

I grabbed his face and pulled it close to mine. I kissed him and ran my hands down his chest.

"I love you Olivia. I can't live without you."

I kissed him more. It was deep and passionate. I pulled away from him and noticed his eyes were glistening. For the first time seeing his eyes water like that didn't give me pangs of guilt. It gave me feelings of joy because I knew it was borne out of happiness and not pain.

"It's bad luck for the groom to see the bride before the wedding," I said playfully.

"Then I'll let you get ready. I'll be in the sitting room when you're ready."

"Okay, I won't be long." I kissed him one last time.

He left me in the bedroom to get ready. I was so happy and overjoyed I could not stop smiling. I took a hot shower and blow-dried my hair. I brushed it out and curled it, then piled it high on my head. I applied light make up and was ready for the dress. I took it out of the garment bag and noticed there was a set of lace underwear and a garter to go with it. I laughed. He had thought of everything. I put it all on and I was ready in no time.

I couldn't believe this was happening. We had eloped to Vegas and I didn't even know it. I loved this. I loathed the thought of a big wedding and having to deal with family. This was perfect, and it was just as it should be. It would be just me and him sharing an intimate moment together, and saying our vows of loyalty. It was all I could have hoped for.

Chapter 58

An hour later Troy and I were in a small chapel and we stood side by side staring into each other's eyes. It was a light hearted ceremony and we laughed a lot. We said the quick vows and sealed them with a long kiss.

That was it. It was done. We were finally married. I felt a rush of relief come over me. I had never been happier than this moment in my life.

We went back to the suite to enjoy the start of our honeymoon. I was surprised and thrilled when we entered. Troy had told the hotel about our marriage and they had prepared the room when we were gone. There were red and pink rose petals on the floor and on the bed. There were candles lit and the room smelled of jasmine. An ice filled bucket had a bottle of champagne sticking out of it and tall champagne glasses next to it. It was romantic and perfect. I jumped up and down in delight. Troy laughed and picked me up and twirled me around. I kissed him and then he said, "Champagne?"

"Yes, thank you."

He poured two glasses and handed me one. Then he said, "To my beautiful wife, for making me the happiest man on the planet."

We clinked our glasses together and drank. Then he walked over to the corner of the room and sat in a chair. I thought that was odd.

Troy stared at me. "What?" I asked. He smirked and looked at me with lust filled eyes.

He said, "Stand up on the bed."

I laughed. I knew exactly what he was doing. It was re-enacting our first time together. I played along.

"But why?" I asked.

"Just do it. I want to admire you from here."

I looked at him then back at the bed. I took my shoes off and climbed on top of the bed facing him. Rose petals surrounded my feet and I felt like a princess. I remembered how the first time we did this I felt so exposed and vulnerable. Now I felt confident and excited. It was a drastic change.

"Good. That's good, now take your dress off, slowly."

I smiled and tried to act coy and scared to take my part in role playing. I unzipped the side of my wedding dress and slipped it over my head. I held it in front of me for a minute covering me.

"Throw it on the ground," he said.

I locked eyes with him and then threw it on the ground on top of the many rose petals that covered the floor. I stood in my white lace bra and white lace panties and garter around my thigh. "Good, keep looking at me. Don't look away. Now take off your bra, slowly."

I continued to stare at him, and reached behind my back and unhooked my bra. He moved his gaze to my breasts and rubbed his rock hard cock.

"Your nipples are perfect," he said.

"Now take of your panties and throw them to me," he said. I was thrilled. He was talking to me the way I liked to be talked to. He was treating me the way I wanted to be treated. He still had this effect on me. Even now that we had been through so much, and now that we were married. We were still on fire.

I grabbed my panties and slowly pulled them down taking them down to my feet. When I came back up I had them in my hand.

"Give them to me," he said in a sterner booming voice. I tossed them to him. He looked up and smiled at me and said,

"You are wet. Your body is ready for me. You want my cock in you so bad. Don't you?"

I nodded my head yes. He smiled and said, "Say it. Say you want my big hard cock inside you."

"I want your big hard cock inside me."

"Well you're going to have to wait, because I want to taste you first. Can I? Can I taste you?"

"Yes," I gasped.

"Lay down on your back and put your feet together. Touch the bottom of your feet together."

I did as he commanded again.

"Mmmm..." He moaned out loud. "I want to taste you so bad."

He stood up and came to the bottom of the bed. He grabbed both of my feet in his hand and pushed them up toward my center, spreading my thighs apart. He grabbed the garter on my leg between his teeth and then let it go. It snapped back against my leg. He groaned at the sight of it. He lowered his head, and then stuck his tongue out and licked me. I screamed out. He went to work licking every inch of my center. His tongue was inside of me, penetrating me.

"I want you to come in my mouth," he said between licks. "Are you ready to come in my mouth?"

"Yes, yes make me come. I want to come in your mouth."

He applied pressure with his tongue moving it from side to side. With this maneuver, I came. I yelled out, as he moved his mouth down to my opening.

He moaned as he drank. My entire body was tingling and shuddering.

He unzipped his pants and took out his enormous cock.

"I'm going to fuck you. I'm going to fuck you hard," he said.

He reached down and grabbed his shaft and placed the tip in my opening.

"I wish you could see this view," he said. He moved the tip of it in a little more, but not entirely. Slowly he pumped his body forward. I spread my legs apart wider. I wanted it, and I was so wet I knew it would feel like heaven when he slid in.

He looked up at me and with one hard thrust drove his entire cock inside of me. I screamed.

He went deep inside of me. He smiled at me and then grabbed my hips, "You're so wet. You're so tight."

He moved in and out me.

"You're beautiful," I said in a whisper. He looked at me with a grin and said, "I know."

Wrapping his lips around my nipples, kissing them and sucking on them. He said my name over and over as he did so. "Olivia, Mmm...Olivia."

He grabbed my leg and propped it on his shoulder and moved deeper inside me. He thrust harder and harder inside me. Then finally he tensed up and moaned louder and louder, then he came. He collapsed on top of me and I felt the full weight of his strong body. In no time at all we both fell asleep.

I awoke in the middle of the night in a panic. I was having a nightmare about being lost in the woods. It took me a minute to remember that I was safe. I was in the bed next to Troy. I was his. I was his wife and now nothing would ever come between us. My panic subsided and moved closer to him on the bed. He picked up his arm and wrapped it around me. I placed my head on his chest and listened to his heart beat. I felt secure and comfortable. I would never again have to doubt his love for me. I would never have that anxiety or worry. Now it was a definite thing. I allowed myself to relax in his arms. I knew it would take my mind some time to get used to this, but eventually the nightmares would go away.

The next day we left for the airport once again.

"Are you going to tell me now where we are going?" I asked. All the drama was behind us now and things really were wonderful. Troy and I loved each other. After all we had been through, it only made us stronger, and now nothing could tear us apart.

Troy smiled. "How does Paris sound?"

From the Author: Thanks so much for reading COLLIDE, I hope you enjoyed it.

If so, you might like INDULGE, another steamy romance from my Bad Boy Billionaires series.

Read on for a preview.

INDULGE

Indulge yourself ... *with another scorching billionaire erotic romance in Ella Adams' Bad Boy Billionaires series.*

When Kate moves from the US to London, hoping for an exciting new life and more exhilarating experiences, an encounter with cocky billionaire James Lancaster encourages her to indulge her true passions - in more ways than one.

Should she trust this arrogant, but devastatingly sexy man who's obviously used to getting exactly what he wants?

Especially when the very sight of him inspires a sensual side to Kate that she had no idea even existed....

INDULGE *is out now.*

1

Having spent all my life in the U.S, moving abroad had always been a fantasy. I longed to explore enchanting European cities and exciting places.

When I got the opportunity to study abroad, I chose London at the drop of a hat. I'd expected it to be a welcome change from my small town normal life, but I had no idea just how ... exhilarating an experience it would turn out to be.

I had a flat in Bloomsbury - very small, as this area was one of the most expensive places to live in the city. However it was near the university so I was able to find student accommodation.

It was also near the British Museum where I would be spending most of my time.

The museum is one of the most prestigious in the world, and once you go there, it's easy to see why.

It holds the absolute best of everything from the antiquities world, even a full sized Greek Temple within its walls. The temple, reassembled inside the museum and was quite a sight.

Even the building itself was set in an old estate built around the 1600s. It was grand and took up an entire block. The place was so vast it took several days to see all that was housed inside.

The galleries were laid out in a maze and you needed a map to get through it. There were several floors, but I was mostly on the second floor. This is where the staff had their offices and where the research labs were.

I was lucky enough to have received a grant, and a few months of lab time at the museum. I was beyond excited.

This would be my life for the next six months. It was the greatest thing that had happened to me, and that's not saying much when you come from a small town like I did.

Nothing big happened there.

Everyone knew everyone, and for the most part stayed in the town after graduating high school. Even those that went to college still came back to the town to live out their mundane and boring lives.

But I couldn't do that. I needed something more. I needed excitement. I needed to see the world. To experience new things and people, and I wanted to be surrounded in a place thick with history.

London was definitely a good place for that. Every single building there was older than anything in America.

I absolutely loved it. I had been working at the museum for three weeks now, and was finally feeling settled in.

I understood the bus and tube systems, was getting used to the bad coffee and even started drinking tea instead.

Each day was capped by a walk to the museum in the morning where I would breathe in the rich history of my surroundings, and then had the same experience on the walk home.

All the walking was good for me and I could already feel the effects it was having on my bottom and thighs. This was about the extent of my existence in London but I was so happy with it.

I figured it couldn't get any better than this.

2

The following day I was in the lab, late in the evening.

I was alone, or so I thought.

I was eagerly working on my project, and studying an ancient Egyptian piece of papyrus housed at the museum. It was a scroll from the Book of the Dead.

"Who are you? What are you doing here?" A booming voice suddenly appeared from nowhere.

I was immediately startled and nearly jumped out of my skin. I turned looking for the source of the voice, but couldn't see anyone in the dark lab.

"I said, who *are* you?"

"I'm Kate. I'm a graduate student, studying..."

"I see," the voice replied in a thick growl, and an English accent.

I turned toward the high bookcases that stood like a labyrinth in the lab. There, a tall broad figure lingered in the dark.

"I'm sorry, who are you exactly?" I asked.

He emerged from the shadows and I caught my breath.

His dark hair and green eyes were stunning. His sculpted face was shadowed by a thin beard, and his body was that of a professional athlete. I swallowed hard.

He started walking toward me slowly, looking me up and down. He did not hide that he was checking me out, and I suddenly felt like I was naked.

It scared me, but also made me a little aroused at the same time. It had been some time since I'd felt that way.

"What do you have there?" His voice a little softer now, he motioned to the papyrus I had under the microscope.

"The Book of the Dead." I took one step backwards as he came toward me.

He stopped and sighed, then pushed his hand through his hair. He was acting as if I had just said something sexual to him, instead of something scholarly.

Maybe they were one and the same to him.

"It's for my thesis." I was shaking as I spoke.

Now he was standing next to me, towering over me. I was only 5'3 and very petite. His green eyes looked down at me. I inhaled his manly scent, and it was intoxicating.

Then he said,

"So ...Kate. I'm James. James Lancaster."

He reached up to my glasses and slowly pulled them off my face and placed them on the table. He grabbed my hair and undid the bun at the back of my head letting my long dark hair spill on my shoulders.

My breathing grew heavy. I could not pull my eyes from him. He was the sexiest man I had ever laid eyes on. He moved his face closer to mine, leaning down toward me, brushed his lips from right to left against mine, then pulled his face away from me. It wasn't a full kiss, just a brush.

Then he turned his back to me and walked out. I stood there, stunned, motionless, paralyzed, and confused.

What the hell had just happened?

I tried to continue on with my work but it was too late and my mind was a mess. I gave up about an hour later and decided to just go home.

Still, I fantasized about the mysterious stranger called James Lancaster all night and finally had no choice but to pleasure myself while thinking about him.

Only then could I sleep.

3

The next day I grabbed a drink at the truck outside the museum steps and sat at an outdoor table. I was still thinking about the mysterious James Lancaster.

Before I came to London, I was fed up. The same people, the same places, and the same men, and I wanted out.

I needed new experiences. I wanted something to shake my world and to be out of the ordinary if just for once in my life.

They say, be careful what you wish for, and now I know the meaning of that all too well.

I walked into the museum and something caught my eye that I had not noticed before, the name *James Lancaster* on a plaque on the wall.

The Lancaster Gallery... My mouth dropped.

There was an entire gallery named after this guy? He, or perhaps his family must be prominent figures within the museum system, maybe English nobility, or royalty even.

Despite myself, the thought made me aroused afresh.

I walked into the lab where a few colleagues were working on their projects. They all came in very early to work, but I was the night owl.

I worked best at night because there were fewer distractions - until last night of course.

I exchanged casual greetings with everyone and went over to Peter; he was the head manager of the lab, an older gentleman who was fairly quiet and went about his business.

"I saw a plaque for the James Lancaster Gallery when I walked in, is Mr Lancaster an ex-curator or something?"

He laughed a little. "No Mr. Lancaster is actually the museum's biggest donor. A very wealthy businessman - a billionaire actually - who resides here in the city," he said without even looking up at me, as he was concentrating on his work.

I was glad for that; otherwise he would have seen the astounded look on my face.

A billionaire... I thought to myself. He seemed so young, not much older than me I would say.

But what was billionaire James Lancaster doing in the lab last night? I was about to walk away when I figured this was my only chance to get answers.

"So he's a history lover, I assume? Does he visit here often?"

"Rarely. He has his own key and comes and goes as he pleases. He practically owns the museum. Funds all our educational grants."

"Grants?" I asked.

"Yes, including yours. Be thankful there's a wealthy man who enjoys history and sees value in it. You wouldn't be here otherwise."

I walked away feeling more confused than I had last night.

What in the world was going on? Why had James Lancaster touched me like that? What was he doing here so late?

And why could I not stop thinking about him?

4

I needed more answers. The entire day I couldn't concentrate on my work. So I made a lot of walks around the galleries and to the various coffee stands in and around the museum.

I wanted someone, anyone to tell me more about this mysterious billionaire donor.

But I had to bring it up casually. Every other section of the museum had a volunteer posted, so I went into the Lancaster Gallery.

I lingered near that volunteer and finally asked her.

"James Lancaster? An interesting name."

The volunteer stared at me silently.

Oh no, I thought. Busted. Maybe he had hit on her too?

Maybe it was well known that Lancaster preyed on the women of the museum and anyone asking about him makes it obvious that he has targeted them too. I quickly added: "Most of the galleries are named after what they house, like the Parthenon Gallery."

She smiled. "As our top benefactor, Mr Lancaster obviously has an entire gallery named after him. He donated most of the works in here too. He's very important to the museum, and unlike most wealthy donors, has a true passion for history and antiquities."

"Oh I see. Yes that makes sense. Of course." I said.

That's about as much information I got out of anyone.

So going back to the lab, I did what anyone else would. I googled him.

That was sort of a dead end though.

This guy seemed very private, and the only thing that showed up in online media was if he donated money or carried out other charitable causes.

He never showed up at events, or did the whole red carpet thing.

He was so elusive I could barely find one photo of him online.

I finally gave up my search and realized I had spent way too much time on this and needed to get back to my real research - my work.

I worked in the lab for a few hours, but because I spent all day fumbling around looking for information about James Lancaster, I needed to stay late again.

Though, I suddenly felt a delicious thrill at the notion that he might just show up again.

After everyone had left I went to the ladies room to freshen up.

When I was satisfied with my appearance I went back to the lab and threw myself back into my work.

The hours passed, and as night grew near and the museum shut down, I readied myself for another encounter with the attractive billionaire.

I didn't know if James Lancaster would return, but I so wanted him to.

Then around ten thirty, I *felt* his arrival, was actually aware of his presence even before he uttered my name.

"Kate." I heard his voice say. This time I wasn't startled, but still, it took my breath away.

I turned to him, and said, "Good evening Mr. Lancaster."

He stared at me, and his gaze completely locked me in. His green eyes were so intense when they connected with mine.

There was something about him. It was as if he knew some secret about me that he was keeping - though of course that was impossible.

"Good evening Kate," he finally said.

I really didn't know what else to do or how to react. This kind of visceral reaction to a man was a first for me in many ways.

I got up from my chair and said, "I need to get going soon. Is there something I can help you with?"

The corner of his mouth drew up in a half smile. I immediately knew what he was thinking, and I was thinking it too. My breath grew hot and my insides burned with arousal.

He walked over to me again, just as he did the night before and did the same things.

He looked down at me with hooded eyes, took my glasses off and pulled my hair down from the bun I wore.

Again, he brushed his lips against mine, except this time, fully kissed them.

My knees went weak. I almost collapsed except he put his hand around me to hold me up.

Then he pulled away and said, "There *is* something you can do for me actually."

"Oh?" I said in barely a whisper.

"Indulge me."

My eyes grew wide and my mouth dropped open. "I don't know what you mean...." I startled to fumble my words.

"Yes, you do. I think you know exactly what I mean, Kate and I think you want it as much as I do. So why not indulge ourselves?"

I gasped, but I felt more turned on than I'd ever been in my entire life. *Indulge* .... such an evocative word, and so easy to succumb to an entreaty to do so from someone like the man in front of me.

"But I don't even know you," I protested weakly, though every fibre of my being wanted to fuck him then and there. I was already imagining what it could be like and ...

"Is that a no then?" he asked.

"I..." I barely got the word out as he covered my mouth with his and kissed me. I was lost in it. I was so turned on and already so wet and I didn't want him to stop.

He moved his hand over my breasts and squeezed and massaged them. I moaned loudly. I wanted this. I *needed* this. It had been so long since I'd had sex. And I'd never had sex with a man like this. One so powerful, attractive, and who exuded confidence and danger.

I wanted to experience that, to experience *him*.

The pursuit of such excitement was partly the reason I'd come to London in the first place, wasn't it?

Continue reading INDULGE, out now.

About the Author

Ella Adams loves to write steamy romances about sexy dominant take-charge men who send pulses racing.

Her BAD BOY BILLIONAIRES SERIES includes:

COLLIDE - a scorching romance featuring an irresistible bad boy billionaire that begins with a spilled cup of coffee on the streets of New York.

RIVALS - a sizzling Italian billionaire love triangle featuring not one, but two smoldering bad boys.

INDULGE - a sexy romance about a woman who choses to indulge her heart's desires by sharing TWO billionaires.

RESIST - a heart-stopping romance featuring one truly irresistible bad boy billionaire.

Books are standalone and can be read in any order

Made in the USA
Lexington, KY
29 October 2016